IN THE BEGINNING, before the creation of the World, there was only the Great Being Rujir-Zakurele. Rujir-Zakurele was everything and all there was. But since there was only Rujir-Zakurele, the Great Being was bored and fell asleep. As Rujir-Zakurele fell asleep, the Great Being began to dream.

As Rujir-Zakurele dreamed, the World was created.

Consequently, the World was created on accident and without any manner of plan or purpose. The Great Being let things in its dream World happen as they unfolded, not caring to control any of them. However, within this dreamed World, entities known as "the deities" came to control various aspects of existence, from natural elements to qualities possessed by the humans, who developed complex consciousness and societies.

These deities, in the various games they played with human beings, would sometimes either give them powers or turn them into monsters. Aside from Rujir-Zakurele, who was very tired of everything and did its best to ignore it all, the two most powerful deities were Injal, Deity of Death, and Jajul, Deity of Chaos.

From human souls, Injal created the Deathless—immortal winged, skeletal creatures that fed on human lifespans. In Injal's case, the creation of these monsters was minimal and controlled.

Jajul, being the chaotic entity it was, unleashed a curse upon humanity. Infected humans became Accursed, beings that fed only on human flesh and possessed giant arachnoid appendages that burst out of their bodies. The Accursed were not immortal, but they had accelerated healing and were very, very hard to kill.

In order for the humans to have a chance against the Accursed, the other deities gave certain humans Blessings. However, immense power came with downfalls. . . .

*Tales from the Mythusian Empire
books can be read in any order.*

Also by Remy Apepp

Sand to Glass

THE
BLESSED

by

Remy Apepp

Thinklings Books, LLC
Wickliffe, OH

Thinklings Books
1400 Lloyd Rd. #552
Wickliffe, OH 44092
thinklingsbooks.com

THE BLESSED

PART I: LUX

HE AWOKE TO THE DARKNESS, first and foremost. Next came the sensations of hunger and pain.

When he managed to open his eyelids and blink away the blackness, his gaze met eyes that were blue like the hearts of flame. They seemed to glow in the dimness of the room.

He thought he'd seen them somewhere before, but when he checked his memory, he found nothing there. He couldn't remember anything. Not where he was, nor how he'd gotten there, nor his name or who he was.

The young man with the fire-blue eyes was speaking to him, but it took him several moments before he was able to understand the words.

When comprehension of language returned, he would learn that this young man was named Illiaz Fonhellansicht. Illiaz called him "Lux," which he supposed must be his name, as the nomenclature did not feel wrong. He did not know for certain if it was truly his, but he liked the way it sounded when Illiaz said it. Illiaz had a voice like blood: bright, silky, and warm. It was certainly much warmer than Illiaz's skin, which, when he reached out to brush the hair from Lux's eyes, was frigid.

"Do you remember anything from before?" was one of the first questions he would remember Illiaz asking him.

"From before what?" His own voice was deeper, more textured. It felt strange, vibrating the cords in his throat.

Illiaz's smile was soft, but the blue of his eyes was not. "From before waking up here."

"I don't remember anything before you." Nothing save the darkness, hunger, and pain; but those were things that did not seem worth mentioning.

It was hard to tell if Illiaz was disappointed. He did not seem to be. "I see," was all he replied. "Are you hungry, Lux?"

Lux was.

Something in Illiaz's scent smelled good, but it wasn't the aroma of rose and sandalwood that graced his skin. It was something beneath that.

Illiaz brought him to another room and silently beckoned over a servant, who set a covered metal tray on the dark wood table, then lifted the lid away to reveal a slab of bloody meat.

It smelled bitter and foul.

Illiaz gestured to it gracefully. "Would you do me the favor of trying this for me?"

"Why?" He had no desire to eat something that smelled so putrid.

"I just want to know if it's palatable to you," Illiaz said graciously.

"It's not. I can tell by the smell." Meat that foul would undoubtedly make him sick.

Illiaz looked at him with his flame-blue eyes and smiled apologetically. "I would appreciate it if you would try it for me anyway."

He was reluctant, but he nonetheless acquiesced. He nearly threw the meat up. He would most certainly have done so had he tried to force it down; but as he simply gagged and spat the meat immediately back out, he avoided the digestive upheaval.

He could not remember having ever vomited. But he must have done so at some point, as he knew that it was an unpleasant experience.

Illiaz offered him a glass of water to rinse the fetid taste out of his mouth, and then handed him a handkerchief with which to wipe the foul blood from his lips.

"I'm sorry about that," Illiaz said. "Thank you for your cooperation, though. I won't ever ask you to do that again."

Lux could not get the nauseating taste from his tongue no matter how much he spat. "What was the point?"

"I was testing something," said Illiaz. He waved for the servant to take the offensive meat away. "Please bring the usual." The servant replaced the metal cover and removed the meat from the table.

"What does it mean that that meat isn't palatable to me?" His mouth still tasted disgusting. It made him feel a degree of irritation, but the feeling was muted. In fact, all his emotions seemed dull to the point of being unworthy of attention and regard. It was, therefore, the least troublesome option to ignore them.

Illiaz steepled his fingers. The movement caused the long sleeves of his dark shirt to pull slightly up from his pale, thin wrists. Those wrists were skeletal, the veins an almost lurid blue beneath his skin, similar to the fire of his eyes. "You're sure you don't remember anything?"

"Yes." There was nothing before Illiaz.

"Then that can wait," Illiaz said, as the servant came back in and set a new silver platter on the table.

There was again a bloody cut of meat, but this one smelled delectable. Lux's mouth watered.

"Please, help yourself," Illiaz said, gesturing easily to the platter.

Lux did.

The flesh was both salty and sweet. Lux ate with his fingers, then licked off all the blood. Illiaz handed him another handkerchief to wipe his hands and mouth, which he did obligingly.

Illiaz was watching him, and Lux met his lurid blue gaze, holding it. "What is it that you so badly want to know if I know?" .

Illiaz looked at him for a moment, then away. His hair, which was even paler than his skin, fell into his face and further obscured his already indecipherable expression.

Lux ran his tongue over the pointed edges of his teeth, the pleasant taste of flesh still in his mouth. "What are you trying to protect me from?"

Illiaz laughed lightly. "So blunt," he remarked, with what appeared to be true amusement. "But I'm not trying to protect you from anything, Lux—you're hardly someone who needs protection."

Lux wondered what that meant, and if it had something to do with the chained cuffs around his ankles and wrists. They did not bother him or inhibit him much, but they were still there: a concrete presence, if a rather mystifying one.

Illiaz did not say anything further on the matter, explaining only, "There's simply no reason to force the inevitable," and brushing the matter away with an airy shrug.

Everything about Illiaz was airy, as if he were walking, breathing sky. He reminded Lux of desert wind in his lungs and limitless heights above his head: feelings Lux somehow knew and understood despite having no memories of experiencing them.

"You've told me not to go into the sun." He also knew and understood the idea of the sun, even though he had no memories of it. What with the heavy drapings over the mansion windows pulled closed, and the chandeliers and fireplaces in the rooms always lit, it was as if outside were always night.

Illiaz sighed in response, waving a hand dismissively. "It's complicated, and I don't trust my ability to explain. It'll be much more pleasant for both of us to wait for you to remember on your own." He shrugged casually and smiled. "If, as you claim, you don't remember anything, then what little I could explain wouldn't make sense. Therefore, there's no point in doing so." His voice was weightless, but his eyes had coruscant depths like sapphires.

Lux knew, without knowing how he knew it, that you could drop sapphires into flame and they would not burn, while diamonds would. Sapphires in flame illumed as if they were the hardened hearts of fires themselves, condensed and corporealized.

Lux felt a desire, however muted, to see Illiaz's blue eyes coruscate and gleam where others would burn. "You must know why I'm wearing these." He held up his cuffed wrists. "You could tell me that." He did not know from where he got the knowledge that people tended to scorch, disintegrate, and decay; he did not know why he felt certain that Illiaz wouldn't.

Illiaz's shrug was aloof, indifferent. "Too much effort. If you want answers that badly, hurry up and remember by yourself." His voice was smooth but salty.

There were some things in life that were easy to accept, reconciled unreservedly and unthinkingly: the color of the sky; the existence of hunger; the way that Illiaz was avoiding his gaze. "You resent me for not remembering."

For a moment, Illiaz was still, unreadable as a marble statue: motionless, emotionless, lifeless perfection. The kind that one could not imagine as being real because it was too obviously a work of art.

Then Illiaz's expression cracked. From it emerged the subtle moon-curve of a smile, and he once again moved like a living being with breath and heartbeat. His eyes became fond, even as he admitted, "Maybe I am slightly resentful."

There was a bouquet of flowers on the table. White roses, blue delphinium, white carnations, green button poms, and white lilies were stuck in the vase haphazardly. Illiaz reached out with a hand, brushing pale fingertips softly over the petals. "It's only to be expected that you would have forgotten." As he spoke, he carefully rearranged the flower stems, moving them into more harmonious positions. "Forgetfulness is just as important to survival as memory, if not even more so."

A fire crackled in the fireplace behind Lux, the heat from it palpable in the air. The flickering flames danced light and shadow on the ornate stone walls. Something about all of it was familiar, but something else about all of it felt foreign.

"It might be better if you don't remember," Illiaz said finally, left hand delicately pulling the flowers free, gathering them into his right. "At least, I hope that nothing makes it necessary for you to remember."

Illiaz placed the blooms from his hand into three bouquets, arranging them differently. He placed more of the white roses and lilies in the center bouquet, more of the blue delphiniums and green button poms in the outer ones, such that the three previously individual bouquets became part of a single, complementary flower arrangement. "I'm sure, Lux, that it will be much easier for you to adapt to the world as you are, when you can't remember how you were before."

Illiaz stood back, regarding the flowers with an unreadable expression. Lux watched him, feeling just as enigmatic. "Who are you to me?"

Illiaz's heartbeat stuttered, and the young man stilled. Slowly, as if the flowers in front of him were wild animals he might scare away, he brushed his fingers over one of the lilies. The white bloom shivered at his touch. "...An admirer," he murmured finally. He brushed his thumb over the petal and then pulled his hand away. His heartbeat was back in its even, rapid rhythm.

Lux noted passively the way the firelight illumed the pale lashes of Illiaz's lowered eyes, the fine hairs that were usually invisible on his skin but which the fire behind him created into a thin glowing outline around his darkened profile. His bangs had fallen half dimgray and half glowing-white into his face, casting dispersive shadows.

Lux blinked slowly, torpid and mild. "Then this must be difficult for you."

Illiaz looked over at him, the blue of his eyes somehow never failing to be startling. "It's not, actually," he said. He smiled, light and open as the lilies. "Even now—even like this—you're wondrous." His voice was all aromatic rose, his softly delighted laugh the green button poms.

Yes, the bouquets matched Illiaz, standing out against the dark, red-ochre room of heavy, lasting woods and stone, of purring flames. Against the monumental backdrop, Illiaz, like the flowers, seemed inevitably transient.

The lingering taste of blood was still in Lux's mouth, mingling with the scents of rose and sandalwood. It made Lux feel almost dizzy, and he ran his tongue between his lips as if that might ground him. "Have you often been told by others that you're crazy?"

Illiaz looked at him with fire-soft blue eyes and said, "No."

Illiaz's heartbeat retained its even pace. Lux found his lips curling ever so minutely. "Have I?"

"Often been told that you're crazy?" Illiaz made an elegant gesture, the movement making the blue iridescence of his dark shirt shimmer. "Whether or not that's the case, I wouldn't know."

"What would you say?"

Lux had meant the question mostly in jest, but Illiaz regarded the matter solemnly. "...Neither of us is crazy, Lux," he said, with a finality like night falling. "It's the world that's crazy. And the deities."

Lux found his lips quirking, his amusement like rainfall: cold and impartially ruthless. "Whether or not that's the case, I wouldn't know."

Illiaz averted his gaze. "You will, though," he said. "But it might not bother you any."

In Lux's chest were unnamable emotions. They leapt and subsided like the firelight dancing on the shadowed walls. "I guess we'll see."

"Indeed." Illiaz looked back at him. "You should go rest. You still need to build up your strength."

"I'm stronger than you, Illiaz." Beneath his hands, Lux knew, Illiaz would be crushed like flower petals.

Illiaz's smile only grew. "Not as strong as you have the potential to be." His blue eyes glinted, his expression delighted, or perhaps reckless. "Clearly: since you're not yet strong enough to remember anything."

Lux wondered at how something so delicate could be so sharp.

Then again, even roses had thorns.

Lux closed his eyes, pushing his chair away from the table and rising to his feet. "Very well, I acquiesce." He looked at Illiaz, again meeting his gaze. "But are you not afraid you might regret this?"

Illiaz smiled still wider, blue eyes aglow. "I won't." There was not the slightest hint of fear or doubt in his gaze. It danced like fire, unremitting.

Lux turned to go. "I'll make sure to remember to hold you to that."

"Please do," came Illiaz's smiling voice from behind him. Lux exited the room to the sound of Illiaz pushing his chair: wooden legs sliding over the woven wool rug, wooden arms just barely knocking against the table.

"Stay out of the sunlight, Lux," Illiaz called as he left.

Lux forgot.

The sunlight was warm on his skin, but it scorched him behind his eyes.

HIS NAME WAS Luxanthus Nkidu Madubabakar. He'd been the Second Prince of the desert kingdom of Ordyuk, called a Blessed warrior, and now he was a gladiator in the kingdom of Mythus's Arena, in which fighters and accursed monsters fought each other to the death. He was very, very good at killing the Accursed. How could he have been so good if he was not Blessed with gifts from the deities?

In the barracks, the warriors were organized by level. Luxanthus was housed with the other Monster Killers.

They were all young, like him, and truly excellent fighters. Yet not a single one of them was Blessed.

One of the other Monster Killers was named Tiyrrin. He had

cool-toned olive skin and shoulder-length rabbit-brown hair, strands of which fell into his angular face. He was jumpy and watchful, constantly anxious and fidgeting, his pale gray eyes darting over everyone like he might be attacked at any moment. He often giggled anxiously, a rictus stretched over his face.

When Tiyrrin fought the Accursed in the Arena, with their giant appendages like spiders or scorpions and the whites of their eyes made red with blood, he was wild and desperate—not the fighting of a warrior aiming to kill, but of an animal battling for its life. He excelled at dodging and blocking, but he was sub-par at attacking. His strategy was to tire the Accursed out with his unending nervous energy, wait for them to falter, and then sweep in for the kill. His endurance was phenomenal.

When Tiyrrin wasn't fighting or training, he was pacing or sharpening his weapons. He slept lightly and awakened at a breath, ready and coiled.

To Luxanthus, he seemed like someone more used to being hunted than to killing. After every battle, Tiyrrin sagged with relief, his laughter elated.

When Luxanthus killed the Accursed—clashing against their armored arachnoid appendages, running up them and flipping over them close enough to see the sharpness of their teeth as he chopped off their heads, landing lightly as they flailed in death throes behind him—he felt nothing.

He and the other Monster Killers trained in the same courtyard, and often they trained with each other. But Luxanthus only ever trained with Tiyrrin once. As they were sparring, Tiyrrin suddenly stopped, frozen, his sword dropping from his numbed hands.

Tiyrrin used a straight, two-handed broadsword, while Luxanthus preferred one-handed curved blades with the sharp side on the outside edge. Luxanthus halted those blades in the air, coming to a stop. Tiyrrin's pale gray eyes were wide with fear, and he slowly sank to his knees. "I can't do it," he said, voice weak and shaking. "I can't win. I can't." He trembled and flinched away when Lux offered him a hand to pull him back to his feet.

"This is just sparring," Luxanthus said. "The point isn't to win."

Tiyrrin gave an incredulous laugh. "The point is *always* to win. Winning is everything."

After that, Tiyrrin kept his distance, watching Luxanthus with terror and shrinking away from him, as if he thought Luxanthus was going to try to kill him at any moment. Sometimes, the youth would fly into a panic, turn and flee, or else curl up in a ball, shaking and crying.

"I can't win," he'd sob. "I'll never be able to win."

Luxanthus didn't understand. "I'm not going to hurt you," he tried to tell him.

Giggling in terror, Tiyrrin said hysterically, "That's what everyone says."

"We're both Monster Killers," Luxanthus pointed out. "We're not going to have to fight each other in the Arena."

"Unless one of us becomes a monster," Tiyrrin said.

"I won't," Luxanthus replied, assured.

Shaking, Tiyrrin said quietly, *"I might,* though."

Tiyrrin, before every fight in the Arena, was overcome by his terror of losing to the Accursed and ending up infected, of becoming one of them himself.

Luxanthus Nkidu, before every fight in the Arena, felt nothing.

Then again, he knew that he was going to win. He was such a talented warrior that everyone believed he was Blessed. He'd never get turned into one of the Accursed.

THE HALLS OF THE Fonhellansicht mansion, as Lux walked through them, were dark despite their high-arched ceilings.

They were also lined with suits of leather and metal armor. The suits were torn, twisted, black-stained, and pierced-through, as if they had been taken from mutilated corpses. They lacked their swords and shields—portrayed exactly how they'd died: defenseless, helpless.

The flickering candlelight from the chandeliers gave them the appearance of movement, as if they were shaking with fear. Sometimes they nodded their helmets at him or waved their gloves as he passed, and Lux would nod or wave back.

The mansion was a large and elaborate one. Marble statues of human figures sat atop mantels, stood atop pillars, surmounted the crowning pieces of the grand staircase railings. They were expertly carved bodies of men and women, but all of them were missing their heads or other pieces of their bodies, as if a monster had torn through the halls. Lux wondered what had happened.

When he'd asked, Illiaz had simply smiled at him vaguely and said, "They've always been like that." Lux wasn't sure he believed it.

It could've been because of his lack of memories, but Lux felt that the mansion was odd. The rooms were full of paraphernalia that had no business being in the same company: anything from simple decorative pieces to maps to inexplicable gadgets. There were also murals decorating many of the walls and ceilings: figures of half-naked men and women adorned in clothes and jewelry; well-muscled figures surrounded by light so bright their features were inscrutable darkness; skeletal figures with one or two pairs of feathered wings sprouting from their backs; toned figures with giant arachnoid appendages sprouting out from their bodies.

Some of the scenes looked like somebody's daydream—some of them looked like somebody's nightmare.

The mansion was a strange place, but Lux liked to wander through it, and appeared to be free to do so without restriction. The depictions in paint and stone didn't hold any meaning for him, but he liked looking at them. Something about them calmed him, like meat between his teeth: an assurance that the gnawing emptiness within him would be satiated.

It was mostly silent, although occasionally there was a ringing of distant, indistinguishable echoes. As if remnants of dreams were tailing him, never planning on coming close but never planning on letting him go. Sometimes he saw shadowy figures in the corners of his vision or heard quiet footsteps around him. The presences did not seem altogether benign, but since they never talked to him, never showed their faces, and did not seem eager for confrontation, he ignored them.

With every step, the chains around his ankles and wrists clinked.

"Why do I have to wear these?" He'd asked the question of Illiaz once.

The chains weren't uncomfortable, so he did not particularly mind them. He just wondered whether they had any significant meaning. Neither Illiaz nor the servants wore any such things.

Illiaz, carefully removing the chain from Lux's wristbands for the night, smiled slightly. "So that other people can feel at ease," he answered, kneeling down to remove the chain from the bands around Lux's ankles.

Illiaz's movements, as always, were light and graceful, the touch of his fingers delicate. Lux looked at him kneeling at his feet.

"Other people are scared of me." He said it—thought it—absently. It was merely a conclusion, as would be the solving of a riddle or the assemblage of puzzle pieces.

"Yes," Illiaz answered easily.

"Then they have a reason to be."

"Yes," Illiaz said again, rising back to his feet with the chains in his hands. His rising stirred the air, bringing the scents of rose and sandalwood afresh to Lux's nose. As if that could conceal the warm smell of Illiaz's skin or the salty-savory aroma of his pulsing blood.

Illiaz walked over and set the removed chains on the ornately carved bedside table, its wood leafed in gold. He laid down the two chains on its surface in careful floral designs, before pulling back his hands to regard his work. He adjusted one of the patterns, fixing some apparent flaw.

He had turned his back to Lux easily. "But you're not."

Illiaz turned his head to look back at him, a soft sweeping of lily-white hair and a regarding of eyes that, even in the flickering of candlelight, were a startling blue. "Scared of you?" Illiaz smiled. "No, I'm not."

"Why?"

Illiaz breathed easily, running his fingers over the duvet on the bed. Fittingly, the chambers that were Illiaz's were the lightest that Lux had seen in the entire mansion: soft, silky golds; pearly creams; and satiny mauves. The dark clothes Illiaz wore made him stand out just as starkly here as in the rest of the building, and Lux wasn't sure if he purposefully made himself stand out or if he simply did not care.

Lux certainly didn't mind if the whites, golds, and deep blues he always found himself dressed in marked him as out of place. He felt out of place with everything anyway. Even with himself. He made decisions without knowing why he was making them, without being sure if they were his, and without caring either way.

Illiaz, on the other hand, gave the appearance that his every choice, every word and gesture, was purposefully and artfully calculated. Lux wondered to what end.

"Why do you think people are scared of what they're scared of?" Illiaz asked him, fingers smoothing the wrinkles in the satiny duvet—though the attempt was in vain, given that the covering was sewn to have folds and ripples. "What is it, exactly, that you think people fear?"

Lux ran his tongue along the insides of his teeth. "I don't remember anything. About anything. Should I somehow still know the answer to this?"

Illiaz's lips curled. "I suppose not." He met Lux's gaze with fire-blue eyes. "Ultimately, Lux, what people are afraid of boils down to two things: people are afraid of pain, and people are afraid of death."

"Then if people are scared of me, I have the ability to cause them both pain and death."

"Yes," Illiaz said, smile widening. "You indeed have that capability." He shrugged, gesturing with his pale, spidery hands. "Of course, everyone has that capability, to this or that extent. You just happen to have more of it than others." His smile was vivid and unforgiving. "That was always the case—it's just even more the case now."

Lux wondered if that was why the chains didn't bother him any.

Illiaz's heartbeat had risen slightly; but judging by his expression, that was due to happiness or thrill, not fear.

Lux felt tired. Or maybe he was hungry. "Then you aren't afraid of pain or death?"

Illiaz's laugh was somehow more delicate than his smile. "What is pain?" he asked, before answering his own question: "Pain is just a warning that you could possibly die. It's a part of being alive. Why is it, then, that most people fear pain?" His eyelids lowered slightly, a soft petal-movement of pale white eyelashes. "They fear pain because they find it unpleasant and can't bear it. Because of that, they want to avoid it—or if they can't avoid it, then they want to ameliorate it by some means—and they will do whatever they can in order to do so."

His smile had taken on a certain impression of darkness. "Pain has the power to make people want to die—and that scares them further, because they fear death." He raised a hand, holding up two fingers. "Now, there are two reasons to fear death: One"—he lowered a finger—"is that death is the ultimate unknown; no one knows what happens when you die. People fear the unknown because it has the potential to lead to unexpected pain. The fears become a self-perpetuating cycle, impossible to extricate oneself from." His smile sharpened with lurid sineriness.

He raised his second finger again. "The second reason to fear death is that death is the end of life, and therefore the end of possibility, choice, and action; once you're dead, you can no longer achieve anything."

His expression sobered, smile fading away as he met and held Lux's gaze. "If there's anything that you want to accomplish or experience in your life, death is terrifying because it is the only thing that can prevent you from doing so."

Lux could identify no fear of anything within himself. Both pain and death seemed utterly irrelevant to the state of his existence. He could also think of nothing he wanted.

Illiaz shrugged airily. "Most people aren't that ambitious with what they want to make of their lives. They fear death for the first reason and the first reason only. Even if they don't have a reason to live, they'll do everything they can in order to stay alive, because they fear the unknown of death." He shook his head, pale hair brushing across his face. "Which is again why most people do not have any great ambitions: they fear pain too much to be willing to withstand any amount of it even for the sake of achieving some greater goal."

He met Lux's gaze again, smiling with a complacent secretiveness like snapdragons. "Most people don't have anything they want desperately enough to fear death's ability to keep them from it." He lowered his hands and slipped them into the pockets of his dark pants. Like his shirt, his pants hung loosely on his skeletal frame. "But there are a few who do; and for this latter group of people, once they have either accomplished or experienced that which they have desired—or else lost all chance of doing so—the possibility of dying no longer frightens them."

His lips curved wryly. "In order to accomplish anything great, you have to be willing to suffer pain. Pain as a reminder that you're capable of dying can be terrifying if you don't want to die—but the fact that you're feeling pain means that you're still alive, and therefore is far more a reason for hope and determination than one for misery and desolation."

He turned in the candlelight that was dancing gold over his clothes and skin. "If you've already achieved what you wanted to, you no longer fear death, because death can no longer take the ability to achieve that from you. And if some other reason has taken that chance of achievement from you, you no longer fear death because you feared death only as loss, and you've already lost all that you could care to lose. Therefore"—he shrugged, light as pale petals fallen from cherry blossoms—"death no longer holds any meaning."

Lux felt like an expanse of night, dark and empty except for falling rain, dragging those petals down to the torrents of rushing black water.

"You didn't answer my question, Illiaz. I don't care why other people do or don't fear pain or death." He tried to catch the flame blue of Illiaz's gaze. "What I want to know is why you don't fear being hurt or killed by me."

Illiaz's smile was gone. "...I do not fear pain by your hand," he said finally, "because there is nothing you could possibly do to me that would be more painful than what I've experienced already."

He shrugged, then, giving a gesture that was both elegant and irreverent. "I do not fear death by your hand," he said, with a softness like decay, "because I know that I am going to die at some point, no matter what. Therefore, the fact that I will die is itself meaningless to me. All that matters to me is *how* I die. And if I have to die, being killed by you would be far preferable to most—if not all—other ways I could imagine dying."

Illiaz gave a careless laugh. "If you happened to kill me," he said, "I would die with no regrets."

"Why?" Lux felt like a pillar of stone: unmovable, unshakable, unfeeling, and uncomprehending. Nothing there except a monolith of the emptiness of forever.

"If you kill me," Illiaz said, his own hand at his throat, fingers ghosting over his pulse, "then I won't die alone."

Somewhere along the way, Illiaz's smile had become sardonic, and it was now stretched exposed on his face like a skeleton rotted free of its flesh. "There is always a possibility of death in any circumstance, Lux. I'm not going to avoid climbing up a flight of stairs just because I could die from tripping and falling down them. And I'm not going to avoid you just because you're capable of killing me."

He gestured, derisive. "If you avoid stairs just because falling down them could kill you, you're never going to get any higher than where you are. You'll never be able to see the view from the top, or obtain anything that's up there, or be able to look down at where you once were and see how far you've come."

Lux exhaled. "I wasn't asking about stairs."

Illiaz was expressionless for a moment, and then slowly his lips curved. "For better or for worse, Lux," he said, tilting his head as he regarded him, "our fates are intertwined. As long as one of us is alive, so must the other live. You won't die for as long as you don't kill me; I won't strive to die for as long as you live."

There was a feeling in Lux's chest like stone cracking. "What does that mean?"

Illiaz laughed, colder than death and smoother than bone. "We are each other's prisoners and jailors, Lux. Not everything can be justified. I can't explain why, out of everyone in the world, the deities saw fit to cross our fates."

"But you can explain how these circumstances came to this point, can you not?"

There was a candleholder on the bedside table, curling rose-stems of bronze. The blossoms on each stem sported a cream-white candle. Illiaz passed a finger through one of the flickering golden flames, blue at its heart. "There are different kinds of strengths, Lux. There is a soft power, and there is a physical power. You are peerless in terms of the latter but hopeless in terms of the former. As such, only the former can hold you. As for me, I have plenty of the former but next to none of the latter."

Lux could only blink at him. "Do you try purposefully to be incomprehensible?"

Illiaz said nothing, passing his finger back and forth through the candle flame.

Inside the void of Lux's chest was his heartbeat, steady like viscous liquid slowly dripping. "Are we here because you want me to kill you?"

Illiaz laughed, turning away from the candles. "Not being afraid of you killing me isn't the same thing as *wanting* you to kill me," he said. "Then again, maybe I *do* hope that you'll be the one to kill me in the end—I just don't necessarily hope that that end will be right now." He looked at Lux with crinkles at the corners of his flame-blue eyes. "You do, you know, have a way of making life seem desirable."

Looking at Illiaz, Lux found himself preternaturally aware of his own blinks. The dark streaks of his eyelashes brushing through his vision. "Then you want me to hurt you?"

The fire of Illiaz's smile quieted, faded, and then slipped away. "You already are," he said.

Lux felt buried in stone. "How?"

"Awe and pain are two sides of the same coin," Illiaz said. "And you, Lux, are *unforgivingly* talented."

Lux frowned slightly, his gaze sliding off Illiaz, slipping to the floor and puddling there like drool from a hung-open, salivating mouth.

The rug spread over the stone was ivory in shade, patterned with rectangular borders around a large, intricate floral design. Lux could smell the rug's wool. He could smell, too, the burning wax from the candles, the rose and sandalwood of Illiaz's cologne, and the old blood that someone had tried to wash out of the silk bed sheets. It all blended with the aftertaste of fresh blood lingering in his mouth.

He felt suddenly skewed, disarranged, deranged, as if someone had savagely hacked the world into pieces and then haphazardly tossed it back together so that none of the edges matched up.

"Will I understand once my memories return?"

Illiaz shrugged and said, "Possibly. But possibly not." He looked like a personification of moonlight garmented in swaths of night, but he smelled of living meat and fresh blood.

His smooth tone sounded like he knew everything there was to be known, and yet his words were: "I certainly wouldn't know."

Lux felt like he was falling, blind as if the sunlight were shining straight into his eyes.

HIS NAME WAS Luxanthus Nkidu Madubabakar. He'd been the Second Prince of the desert kingdom of Ordyuk, called a Blessed warrior, and now he was a gladiator in the kingdom of Mythus's Arena, in which fighters and accursed monsters fought each other to the death.

One of the other Monster Killers was called Jyunpey. He had mid-length black hair, gray-blue eyes, a stealthy way of walking, and a wolf's smile. Luxanthus could tell by the way he moved that he was a natural-born killer. When he fought the Accursed, he taunted them and messed with them for a considerable time before finally killing them, seeming to delight in causing them as much pain as possible before the end.

The rumors were that death followed Jyunpey: he didn't even have to touch others to kill them, for they'd kill themselves from his words and actions alone.

Tiyrrin avoided Jyunpey like he was a snake. Jyunpey paid next to no attention to Tiyrrin, following after Luxanthus instead.

Jyunpey liked to talk. He asked questions and made suggestions. He sort of reminded Luxanthus of his sister, Rkalla. She'd always tried to get a rise out of him, too. She'd also always failed.

"How does it feel," Jyunpey asked him, "to be abandoned by your family? To be taken away to another kingdom to fight monsters at the risk of your life, knowing you'll likely never return?"

"Is it different from your situation?" Luxanthus inquired. He didn't know why Jyunpey would be asking, otherwise.

"I'm a criminal," Jyunpey said, smiling like a starved canine and spreading his hands. "Since I was killing, they figured I might as well be doing it for others' entertainment rather than at random."

"How does that feel, then?" Luxanthus wanted to know.

Jyunpey tilted his head, regarding him with narrowing eyes. "It really doesn't bother you?"

"Which part?" Luxanthus asked.

"Being abandoned by your family," Jyunpey said, a curl to his lips. "Being housed with murderers."

Luxanthus shook his head. "It doesn't bother me, no. As long as I can be useful, I don't mind doing what I have to." He was good at fighting. Why shouldn't he want to do what he was good at?

"But surely there must be *something* that you resent about this," Jyunpey insisted. "It's okay to get it out, you know. There's no need to hold it in."

"Then what about you?" Luxanthus wanted to know.

"I prefer to carry out my killing in the dark," Jyunpey said, idly scraping the dried blood from beneath his fingernails. He crinkled his nose. "Having to kill in the light in front of everyone leaves a bad taste in my mouth."

"Whether it's done in the dark or the light, it's the same," Luxanthus pointed out. "The only difference is that for one you're recognized, and for the other you might never be known."

"I'm guessing you're the kind of person who likes acknowledgment," Jyunpey said, eyeing him.

"I guess I'm used to it," Luxanthus admitted.

Jyunpey regarded him dubiously. "You truly don't resent any of them for this?"

"I don't see why I should," Luxanthus said. "We all have roles to fill; I'm simply upholding mine."

Jyunpey's lips curled in a sneer. "Do you even feel anything, or are you dead inside?"

"I kill, but I've never been killed," Luxanthus answered. "That's what makes me a good killer. Like you."

"Can't die if you were never alive, huh?" Jyunpey snorted.

"I'm plenty alive," Luxanthus said, turning his attention to the sword he was cleaning. He was more alive than he would have been had he actually been Blessed, as everyone believed him to be. After all, Blessings came with a catch: the more one used their power, the more quickly it ate away at their life force. True Blessed warriors never lived long.

"And in any case, why do you care?" he asked Jyunpey. "It shouldn't be of any concern to you what I feel or don't; likewise, it's not any of my concern how you feel about the way I am."

"You're inhuman," Jyunpey accused him.

Luxanthus, his lips curving wryly, said, "I suppose I must be, to be able to kill monsters." What other explanation could there be for how he was so good at it?

"You remind me of this dead guy I knew," Jyunpey told him. "He made coffins for the dead because he was more comfortable with them than with the living."

Luxanthus considered this. "Do you mean to suggest that I fight monsters because I'm more comfortable with them than with humans?" He hummed in thought. "You might have a point."

Jyunpey regarded him like a wolf would regard a carcass that had already been gnawed of all its edible flesh.

Lux shrugged and continued wiping the Accursed blood from his blade. People had always believed all kinds of things about him, trying to make sense of what he was.

ILLIAZ'S CHAMBERS WERE on the top floor, and Lux could hear an erratic, unceasing pounding on the stone roof. It was almost loud enough to drown out the sound of Illiaz's soft, moist breathing and the fast, even beating of his blood-wet heart.

"It's raining outside." The realization struck Lux. He remembered rain, or at least he knew what it was, even without memories. He knew what it sounded like, what it looked like, how it felt, what its smells were, how it tasted.

Illiaz, observing him, smiled. "Do you want to go out in it, Lux?" he asked, and gestured with a hand: sweeping, grand, inviting. "We can go out on the balcony."

Lux knew which curtains were covering the connection to the

outside balcony by the smell of wet earth and new foliage slipping through the cracks around the doors. Walking past Illiaz, he pulled the curtains aside and stared into the rain-strewn darkness of night.

"Here," said Illiaz, reaching around him to open the double doors, which swung outward onto the balcony and exposed them to the cold, water-laden air.

Lux stepped onto the wet balcony, chilled stone beneath his bare feet. Shallow puddles splashed water between his toes. He walked over to the railing of the balcony, looking out into the dark. Raindrops, falling heavy and fast, soaked into his hair, trickled down his face and his neck, and saturated his clothes.

Illiaz stood beside him, looking out into the night as well. The raindrops fell in a soft but roaring percussion-serenade of beats and splashes.

The water was cold as it trickled into his mouth. Lux licked it from his lips, then exhaled warm breath. "What if I left?" The color of the night was a comforting darkness. If he leapt over the railing, it would not be deathly far to the ground. He was no prisoner in the mansion; if he wanted to leave, there was nothing that could keep him there.

Illiaz hummed, leaning forward slightly with his elbows resting on the stone railing. His clothes stuck wetly to his skeletal body, his hair plastering to his gaunt face. "If you left, Lux," he said, voice raised slightly to navigate through the pounding of the rain, "where would you go?"

Lux looked out into the darkness, knowing nothing of what lay within it aside from rain, nothing of what lay beyond it aside from the fact that there were other people, none of whom was Illiaz. "Nowhere. Or if I did, I'd probably just come back." There was nothing out there for him.

Beside him was Illiaz, drenched and dripping with rain and yet smiling through the dark. "Yeah," he said, "I figured."

The rain was covering them with kisses, dragging tongues over their skin. Lux shivered. "...It's cold."

"So it is," Illiaz agreed, goosebumps in his voice even as he continued to watch the falling rain.

Lux's clothes and hair were sticking to him, as if with blood, but colder and streaming instead of caking. "And wet."

In the dark beside him, Illiaz laughed. "Indeed."

Lux looked over at him, water falling in streaks between them. "You're shivering." The rain was making the air tremble, but Lux could see Illiaz shaking minutely even through that.

Illiaz met his gaze with eyes fully dilated in the dark, blue eaten up by black. "You're shivering, too, you know," he said, voice nearly lost in the drumming of the rain on stone, on dirt, on leaves, on petals, on fabric, on skin.

Yet even through the rain's symphony, Lux could hear the beating of Illiaz's heart, its tempo raised to try to keep him warm. Beyond him, the darkness yawned wide.

"You should go inside. And take me with you." The rain was like teeth and the darkness threatened to toss him up and swallow him. Maybe he'd fall forever. Maybe it would be relaxing.

Illiaz's voice was light, graceful, and careful. "I'm pretty sure you're capable of going inside under your own power, Lux." It was a voice that dodged raindrops.

The darkness filled his eyes till it felt as if they could spill over, down his cheeks and into his mouth, down his throat and into his lungs till there was no more room for air and the darkness that swallowed him flowed through his veins.

"I feel like I could fall asleep here."

There was an exhale through the rain, followed by the feeling of fingers curling loosely around his wrist. "Come on, Lux."

Illiaz pulled him, and Lux let him, eyes closed until there was once again a roof above his head, the air around him warmed by flames and scented with melting beeswax. He stood there dripping, listening to the sounds of Illiaz shutting the doors and drawing the curtains, the sounds of their clothes dripping water to the floor.

He heard Illiaz peel off his socks and walk barefoot to the bathroom, grab some towels and then return; heard the sound of the towel moving through the air, and automatically reached up and caught it before it hit him in the face.

When he opened his eyes, towel in his hands, Illiaz was there in the candlelight with a towel draped sideways over his head, a curl to his lips. "You're really something, you know that, Lux?"

"No. I don't know anything." He watched Illiaz begin toweling himself off, starting with his hair and then moving down over his face and neck. His dark blue shirt stuck so closely to his skeletal frame that the candlelight was able to play on the arches of his ribs, shadows collecting in the concave depressions between the bones. In the dim candlelight, he was all ashy smudges of light and shadow, as if he were drawn in charcoal that could be brushed away with a touch.

"Fair enough," came Illiaz's response, as he patted the towel around the pants clinging to his thin legs, as strands of pale, damp hair fell into his face. "And yet, even then."

"Even then what?"

Illiaz glanced over at him, blinking, his bright blue eyes first following the trails of water Lux was dripping and then rolling in their sockets. He took the towel from Lux's hands and tossed it over Lux's head.

"A bird will always have feathers and wings but no teeth, Lux," he said, longsuffering exasperation in his voice as he began gently toweling off Lux's hair. The action made Lux scrunch up his eyes. "A snake will always have scales and no legs but piercing fangs. No matter where they are or where they have or haven't been."

Illiaz dropped the towel down around Lux's neck. "Unless you cut off the bird's wings or pull the snake's fangs." Dark hair had fallen damply into Lux's face and gotten into his mouth. He pulled the strands from between his lips, spitting slightly to get the hair and its acrid taste from his tongue.

Illiaz made a face and wiped away the droplets of spit Lux had gotten on him. He made to reach for a handkerchief, only to realize he had no handkerchiefs on him. He sighed, wiping his hand on his wet pants, even as he replied, "You can take a bird's wings or a snake's fangs, Lux, but you can't add anything that wasn't there. You can cripple them, but you can't change what they are." He shrugged, picking his damp towel up off the floor. "You can't give a bird fangs or a snake wings."

He looked at Lux pointedly. Lux realized he was supposed to keep toweling himself off and moved to do so. "Doing that would create a dragon, wouldn't it?" He knew what birds, snakes, and dragons were, without any memories of having seen any.

Lux tried and failed to extricate himself from his wet shirt, which was confusing him. He couldn't remember having put it on and was uncertain how it worked. It didn't seem to be the same as Illiaz's. Furthermore, it was sticking to his body and seemed like it might take some of his skin off with it. Then there would be blood all over the floor.

Illiaz looked at him with a slight raise of his eyebrows and a quirk of his lips. "A bird with teeth or a snake with wings would be a completely different being, yes," he said, and stepped closer to help Lux free of his wet clothes.

Illiaz seemed unconcerned by Lux's confusion regarding the garment, so perhaps his difficulty with it was normal.

"The point is, Lux, that you can't change who someone intrinsically is," Illiaz continued, taking the wet garments and tossing the towel at Lux again. Lux caught it. "Even if you remove the wings from a bird, it will still be a bird; even if you remove the fangs from a snake, it will still be a snake. And neither of them will ever be a dragon; and a dragon could never become a mere bird or a simple snake."

"That makes sense." Lux wiped the water from his muscled arms, shoulders, and torso. "But I'm not sure what it is you're trying to say."

Illiaz's lips were still curved upward, the blue of his eyes aflame in the candlelight. "Even without your memories," he said, "you're still really something, Lux."

Lux looked back at him, wondering. "To you, it seems." He did not seem to be anything to himself, as vacant and numb as he felt. He couldn't so much as figure out the clothes he was wearing. Talk about inept.

And yet Illiaz just smiled at him softly and said, "Yes."

Lux tilted his head. "But without my memories of you, you're not anything to me."

"Maybe I'm not to you what I once was," Illiaz said, breaking Lux's gaze easily, fingers fumbling with the buttons of his sleeve, "but I'm still *something* to you, am I not?"

"There isn't exactly anyone else in my life at the moment, so I guess so." He watched Illiaz shiver. "But are you to me what you want to be?"

Illiaz gestured gracefully, grandly, almost gloatingly. "I'm in your life, aren't I?"

Lux could only stare at him. "…You must be crazy."

Illiaz brushed a hand back through his hair. "Given that you don't have any memories," he said, moving the hand away in a flippant gesture, his bangs falling limp and damp back into his face, "I don't think you have enough idea of normality to make that assessment."

"Fair enough." Lux looked up at the ceiling, raising a hand to cover his right ear; sometimes it felt like someone was trying to whisper something there. "I guess what I meant was that I don't understand you, Illiaz."

Illiaz let out a huffing exhalation through his nose. "Nobody truly understands anybody else, Lux," he said, waving a hand dismissively. "Most of us don't even understand ourselves."

Lux felt his lips pull slightly away from his teeth. "I certainly don't." He wasn't sure if the expression on his face was a smile, a grimace, or something else.

The curl of Illiaz's mouth split his face open into a grin. "At least you're honest about it," he said, somewhere between mirthful and sardonic. "Most people do so like to live in denial. But you..." He laughed slightly. "You've never been one to run or hide from any kind of difficult truth."

Lux felt the brush of his eyelashes against the skin stretched beneath his eye sockets. The flesh, as he moved his fingers there, was slightly puffy, as if he hadn't been sleeping. "Why would anyone do that?"

Illiaz's eyelids lowered slightly, the curve of his lips softening. "Because most of the time the truth hurts," he said.

"So?"

Illiaz raised a pale eyebrow. "Most people don't like pain, and want to avoid it," he said. "We've already been over this, Lux."

Ah, right. Lux looked up at the dark ceiling, as if it might be easier to collect his thoughts there. "I mean, I understand that, but I don't think that denial is the best way to deal with it. Is pain not just information telling you that something isn't right and needs to be fixed?"

Illiaz's smile was thin: not a supple flower, but a frangible twig. "Maybe some things can't be fixed, Lux."

Lux found that gaze hard to hold and looked away, giving a shrug. "I suppose I wouldn't know. It just seems to me that there's always some choice that could make things better in some way."

Illiaz, utterly inscrutable, laughed at him. "Your life philosophy is impossible."

"How so?"

"It's just amusing," Illiaz said, his eyelids lowering. "And it makes me curious."

Lux placed a hand against his face to keep his head propped up on his neck. "About what?"

"Why don't you kill yourself, Lux?"

Lux blinked at him. "Why should I? Death is the only thing you don't need to do anything to accomplish." The chuckles crawled up from his stomach like scorpions from under a lifted rock. "If you want anything in life, you need to work for it, because if you don't work for it, then it will never happen—except for death. Death will happen no matter what. Whether you work for it or do everything you can to avoid it. So it doesn't make any sense to do either." Lux shrugged. "Death can and will happen all by itself. So why not let it?" He grinned without understanding why. "If I don't need to help it out, then I'm not going to."

It felt like a truth that had long existed inside him, and he'd simply stumbled upon its hiding place.

Illiaz had covered his mouth with a hand and was looking at him with widened blue eyes.

Lux looked back and faltered, the glow of his discovery fading. "What?"

Illiaz's entire body was shaking. "...Only you, Lux," he managed weakly. It became clear that he was trying to restrain his laughter, his words unsteady and muffled behind his hand. *"Only you* could make staying alive sound like an act of *laziness*, of all things."

"I just really don't care any..."

Illiaz's eyes, he saw now, were glimmering not just with candlelight but with water. What he'd thought was strangled laughter was starting to sound more like shuddering sobs.

A pit yawned open in Lux's chest. "...Why are you crying?"

Illiaz choked out, *"You..."* He wiped at his eyes with the back of a hand. When he removed his other hand from his mouth and met Lux's gaze, it was with a ludicrous grin and tears trickling in glistening streams down his pallid cheeks. "Life isn't fair," he said, and laughed, one arm wrapped around his waist as if to keep himself from falling apart. His other hand rubbed furiously at his crying eyes. "Life really isn't fair."

Lux watched Illiaz giggle and sob. He breathed in the salty scent of Illiaz's tears and exhaled softly. "How do you mean?" There didn't seem to be any point in crying about something which was that evident and absolute.

"It hurts, is all," Illiaz said, wiping at his tears and grinning at him. He laughed again, like it was truly hilarious. "It really hurts."

Somewhere in Lux's mind were memories of the sun being warm on his skin, and yet scorching him behind his eyes.

HIS NAME WAS Luxanthus Nkidu Madubabakar. He'd been the Second Prince of the desert kingdom of Ordyuk, called a Blessed warrior, and now he was a gladiator in the kingdom of Mythus's Arena, in which fighters and monsters fought each other to the death.

Out of the Monster Killers, he was not the only one who had previously been a prince. There was an archer by the name of Velurid who had, before becoming a gladiator, been the prince of the military kingdom of Hahsin.

Luxanthus had heard about the difficulty of warrior training in the kingdom of Hahsin, but he was still surprised by the number of Velurid's scars. Luxanthus, for his part, despite all his fight experience, had next to no scars. It was almost certainly part of why no one could believe he was human.

Velurid caught him staring at his scars and his lips twitched ironically. "Unlike Kayds's," he said, referring to the other Hahsinian gladiator, "mine are all self-inflicted."

"Why?" Luxanthus asked him.

Velurid exhaled. He had a warm, copper skin tone, dark brown hair, and yellow-brown eyes. He was long-limbed and lean, with a jackal-like look to him and a dark aura. "Because everything in my mind hurts," he stated. "I hurt myself physically to make the pain in my head stop."

Luxanthus crinkled his brow, trying to imagine that. "And does it help?"

"Yes," Velurid said. "It does." He flexed and stretched his fingers, scratching his nails over the skin of his arms. "Aside from utter exhaustion, it's the only thing that helps."

Luxanthus didn't understand. But there were times when Velurid panicked, repeating "Ow" over and over again as he clenched his fingers in his hair. "Someone hit me," he'd entreat. "Someone make it *stop.*" He'd hiss and whimper, cursing under his breath, pressing the heels of his palms hard against his eyes.

Luxanthus, not wanting his fellow warrior to be left in such a state, would walk over and punch him in the face.

As Velurid was knocked to the ground, a hand going to his split lip, he'd look up at Luxanthus with gratitude and relief.

"Thank you," he'd say through the blood.

"You're welcome," Luxanthus would reply.

Lux would be left wondering why he felt worse for hitting the youth who wanted to be hit than he did for killing the monsters that didn't want to be killed. But since nobody else seemed willing to inflict on Velurid the physical pain he desired, Luxanthus took the duty upon himself.

There was no point in avoiding what was required or desired of him. If everyone expected him to be inhuman, whether a Blessed or a monster, he might as well live up to their expectations.

The only part he'd fail was that he wasn't going to die.

ILLIAZ WAS STANDING AGAIN. There were tearstains on his face, but he was no longer crying. His smile was once again soft, warm, collected, and elegant as the bud of a rose.

"Here," Illiaz said, smiling gently from between the fingers of the hand placed spiderlike over his face, his other holding out carefully folded garments that were clean and dry. "Go take a bath and change your clothes."

Lux took in the goosebumps covering his pallid skin, as well as the look in his eyes that said he was unwilling to compromise.

Exhaling, Lux took the garments, tucking them under an arm. "Right."

He turned, heading to the bathroom to do as he'd been told. He'd bathe and change first, even if Illiaz was colder than he was. There was no point in trying to argue.

By that point, it had become more than clear that Illiaz's care for him was an immutable fact of his reality; the same as his memory loss, the rain that had saturated him, and the candles that provided the room's only light. It was not necessary to know why— only that it was true, and that it was tangible enough to believe in, trust in, and base his decisions and actions on. He would trust Illiaz's care for him the same way he trusted the ground to remain solid beneath his feet, trusted that he would wake up again after each time he fell asleep, trusted that the room existed on the other side of the door even when the door was closed.

Indeed, if he couldn't trust Illiaz, there was not anything that he could trust in the entire world. Nothing else existed for him. He didn't even know himself—not who he was before losing his memories, not who he was now, not even what he looked like. He was a hazy, indeterminate figure, even in his own mind.

He had not come across any mirrors in his wanderings of the manor—and in truth he didn't remember what mirrors were and so had not thought to look for them. His sense of his face came only through glimpses of his reflection that he caught in basins of water: within mugs, small pools at the bottom of sinks, filled tubs before he stepped in—and then again afterward, once he'd stopped scratching his maddeningly itching, squirming flesh, and the bloodied water around him had stilled.

What he saw there was that he was all of varieties of marble: skin of mid-toned brown-gold; fingernails and toenails of solid black; hair of streaked dark brown; eyes of cream-toned yellow with cracks of white and red threading through. All of him chiseled and hard, not at all likely to break.

He stepped out of the warm water that dripped from his marble surfaces in reddish-clear torrents, not a blemish left marking his hard, brown-gold skin. He grabbed a towel, wiping the water from his body and drying his hair until it fell only damp rather than dripping into his face. Then he changed into the clothes that Illiaz had chosen for him, all whites and golds and deep blues.

He walked out, idly scraping the bloodied skin from beneath his black marble fingernails with his teeth. "Your turn."

Illiaz brushed by him, his bones looking like they might tear through his flower-petal skin. Lux watched him disappear through the door and wondered if he'd disintegrate in the water.

But then again, if he hadn't disintegrated in the rain, he probably wouldn't disintegrate in the bath, so Lux decided not to worry about it. If Illiaz came apart like a bouquet in the water, all white petals veined with red and oozing blood from every crushed fiber...well. Beautiful things weren't made to last. Monumental things might last—monumental architectures carved from everlasting, lifeless stone, like castles, pyramids, statues, and Lux himself—but nothing as delicate and alive as blossoming flowers or Illiaz.

Alone in the bedroom, Lux swallowed around nothing; dry air and the tasteless wet of saliva. Inside him was a profound, echoing hollowness, yet it was difficult to call that emptiness hunger; he was starving like stone, which could not feel sated no matter how much it enveloped, crushed, and fossilized within itself.

The emptiness was somehow terrible, and the smell of blood overpowering. Blood, and the essence of rose petals. The former made him salivate; the latter made him gag. Clearly, there would be no peace for him here. Which meant his only option was to attempt to seek peace elsewhere.

He left the room, heading for the kitchen. He wanted to stuff himself full, even if it would not satiate him.

"Make sure you stay out of the sunlight, Lux," Illiaz had told him.

He forgot.

The sunlight was warm on his skin, but it scorched him behind his eyes.

HIS NAME WAS Luxanthus Nkidu Madubabakar. He'd been the Second Prince of the desert kingdom of Ordyuk, called a Blessed warrior, and now he was a gladiator in the kingdom of Mythus's Arena, in which fighters and accursed monsters fought each other to the death.

One of the other Monster Killers was known as either Aiyler or Renz, depending on which personality was in control.

Despite the fact that they shared a body, Aiyler and Renz were unmistakable for each other. The ways they carried themselves, moved, and spoke could not have been more dissimilar. Aiyler slumped and spoke softly while Renz was a fireball of furious energy that erupted everywhere like an active volcano. Even their eye color changed, with Aiyler's appearing more green while Renz's appeared more brindle; and they wore their hair differently, Aiyler letting his dark brown locks fall into his face while Renz tied them back with a leather string Aiyler kept around his left wrist.

It was a stimulating exercise to spar with them, because they'd switch control back and forth, and their fighting styles would change accordingly. It kept Luxanthus on his toes.

Aiyler, despite seeming to be the dominant personality, was lazy and against exerting effort. He found fighting Luxanthus to be annoying, exhausting, and not worthy of time. Meanwhile, Renz had a furious obsession with being the best, and he challenged Luxanthus whenever he saw him.

"I'll beat you this time, desert spawn! I'll show you how we do it in the city back alleys!"

After the first few times Luxanthus and Renz fought, Aiyler stopped allowing it. "You're just going to get your ass beat by him, Renz," he muttered to himself. "Then you're going to push your beat-up body onto me and make me deal with it. It's annoying."

After that, Aiyler would cringe and cover his eyes every time he saw Luxanthus—supposedly because Renz was yelling in his head. It was the only time Luxanthus ever saw Aiyler cringe. Aiyler, unlike Renz, didn't register pain.

"Sorry," Luxanthus would say, because he wasn't sure what he could do. It wasn't his fault that they weren't as good of fighters as he was. Nor was it their fault that he was better than they.

"Just leave me alone; don't speak," Aiyler would groan at him darkly. "You're annoying. You draw out the worst in him. Don't even talk to me."

So Lux would shut his mouth and leave.

He'd never wanted to be anywhere he wasn't wanted. He only wanted to be where people wanted him to be.

He liked fighting in the Arena, for that reason: the crowds cheered for him. They wanted him there. They appreciated his being there and doing what he did best.

He supposed he was just like the Accursed, in that way. In the Arena was the only place that anyone was happy to see him.

THE MEAT LUX FOUND wrapped in the ice chest burst fresh and wet in his mouth, sweet salty juices slipping down his throat with the muscle, a pleasant tender firmness between his teeth. It wasn't nearly enough, so he licked the blood from the cloth it had been wrapped in. When that wasn't enough, he chewed on the cloth. When that still wasn't enough, he made himself a cup of coffee.

Lux heard Illiaz's footsteps long before the young man entered. When Illiaz finally did, he smelled of water, clean clothes, warm flesh, and dry flowers. He had purple in his hair, indigo in his eyes, and violets held delicately between his long fingers. His shirt was mauve with embroidery of gentle lavender, his slacks the deepest color of a fresh bruise, and his shoes like the night sky stained with starlight. His smile was forget-me-not even as he tucked a morning glory behind the pale curve of his ear. Each time he blinked, his eyelashes drifted like bright petals in a sunlit breeze.

Oh, Lux thought, a feeling behind his eyes like the soft nip of snapdragons over his fingertips: So this was what they'd meant when they'd told him that Illiaz Fonhellansicht was impossible to look away from.

Somehow, Lux had expected him to be wearing red, not purple. Now, he wasn't entirely sure why.

Illiaz was looking at him with bloomed cornflower-blue urgency, almost painfully lurid on the eyes.

Lux wanted to turn his large mug upside down over Illiaz's head to see if he'd lose his surreal quality when dripping with coffee. But there was a squirming and crawling in Lux's ears, a droning cacophony in his head, the world slow like he was underwater except that he could breathe, and he wondered if maybe it wasn't Illiaz who was skewing reality.

He glanced around the room as uncertainty crawled up his throat, over his eyes. Everything was almost blindingly bright, like it was lit by morning sunlight instead of a few candles. He wondered if that was Illiaz's doing, or if it was his own mind again. Perhaps a problem with his vision.

There was an odd tugging of the petal-thin skin around Illiaz's eyes, showing the delphinium-blue veins threading underneath, even as he reached out to lightly touch Lux's shoulder.

Lux stared at Illiaz's hand, surprised at its solidity; he'd expected it to pass right through him, like a ghost.

He felt that something inside him was being chased, accosted, like the shadows of night fleeing before the light of dawn only to find themselves caught against a stone wall with nowhere to go or hide.

He felt like he was being burned away against that wall, turning to ash in the heat of the sun. But Illiaz's hand on his shoulder was neither warm nor cold.

He had the thought that he could bite Illiaz's fingers off.

He wondered, if he did, if Illiaz would bleed purple—as purple as the rest of him. Illiaz was certainly not normal. Lux wondered if pain would chase the indigo from Illiaz's eyes, and if heady rose-red would stain the cold lupine of his lips, were he to be stabbed through the chest. He looked like he was freezing, as if he were losing blood and along with it all his heat.

Illiaz moved his hand from Lux's shoulder to his forehead, like he was feeling for a fever. The skin around his eyes pulled further, those not-red lips pursing. Even that movement was languidly graceful on him, like a flower stem bowing slowly under the weight of its blossom. Lux wondered at Illiaz's delicacy, feeling suddenly confused; he thought he could recall that he'd heard somewhere that Illiaz was powerful—terrifying, even—yet here he was, all flowers. All he'd ever been was flowers.

Lux couldn't think of anything that was powerful or terrifying about flowers. Maybe they obstinately raised their heads to stare the sun in its face, but they so quickly withered and died, shriveling and leaning, falling and fading to the ground where they were crawled over by insects and arthropods—ants, beetles, spiders, scorpions, centipedes, millipedes. Crushed beneath the oh-so-many legs that ground them to powder.

Lux didn't realize that he was sniggering hysterically until Illiaz pressed a graceful hand over his mouth, as if he were handing him a flower bouquet—his thumb brushing over Lux's lip, as if he could tie a ribbon there closed. Illiaz was mouthing words, and the indigo was welling up in his eyes, dripping dark trails down his elegant, lily-petal, chiseled cheeks. Lux couldn't hear him, but he somehow knew that Illiaz was begging him to pull himself together.

He couldn't stop snickering, though, the sound crawling out from inside him and turning to laughter, making him writhe like a corpse squirming with maggots—and the indigo was streaming down Illiaz's cheeks and dripping from his chin.

Lux bit Illiaz's hand, driving his teeth into the flesh till the taste of lavender flooded his mouth and bones crackled like dried leaves.

With his teeth embedded deep in the flesh of Illiaz's hand, Lux wasn't laughing anymore. When he looked at Illiaz's face, he saw Illiaz's eyes were inversed red poppies, and he was smiling.

Lux unclenched his jaw from Illiaz's hand, taking a step back, watching him. The poppies' dark roots were growing over Illiaz's pale skin. Lux was trembling, though he didn't know why. He watched him.

Illiaz raised his limp, bloodied hand, and licked the dripping red. Despite the taste of lavender overwhelming Lux's senses, the blood was red, and when Illiaz swept his tongue over his lips, it left them red, too.

The room was oddly silent, like they were standing in an expanse of snow, and Lux wondered where the rain had gone. When it had stopped pounding on the roof floors above them.

When Lux looked around, he saw that the room was not only empty and deserted; that the tables were splintered and overturned, the chairs smashed at the bases of the walls, blood everywhere. Outside the windows, it was dark. The floor was tiled with black and white squares, like a game board. He wondered who were the pawns. Who was the one playing the game and moving the pieces. He wondered which role was his and which was Illiaz's.

Something was unfurling in his chest like a butterfly from its chrysalis. Twirling. Dizzying. What had happened here? Why couldn't he remember anything? There was a hole in his head, and all his memories had spilled out like sand.

There was a keening noise, and he started. It had been so quiet.

He looked around at the broken, empty room. Illiaz was still there, white hair wilting in his face. He was even thinner, withered like a mummy. He was on his knees on the floor in a puddle of dark maroon blood, surrounded by scarlet poppy petals, and his tears were as bright as his eyes. He raised a hand toward Lux—the broken one, the one that Lux had bitten—and he was trembling and pale like snowbells as he mouthed something.

Lux shook his head; he didn't understand what Illiaz was trying to say. Why didn't Illiaz just speak? Surely his voice had to work. His throat was intact.

Illiaz looked like his heart was breaking, which Lux thought was strange, because considering the gaping hole in Illiaz's chest, he shouldn't even have a heart at this point. Yet he still looked ethereal, still made more of flowers than flesh, and Lux remembered the way he tasted of lavender, of lavender, a bitter aftertaste following a flower sweetness.

When Lux shifted his stance, he stepped in something wet. Looking down, he saw that there was coffee on the floor, as well as blood. He felt a warm drop of something fall onto his cheek and run over his skin, all the way down to his chin, where it trembled for a moment before falling. He watched the drop of red fall, splashing into the dark mix of blood and coffee on the floor.

He looked up, meeting Illiaz's gaze. Illiaz tried to mouth something at him again, but started coughing violently, covering his mouth with a pale hand, red slithering wetly through his fingers.

The liquid brimming in Illiaz's eyes was also red, dark as it dripped down his cheeks, caking in his eyelashes.

Removing his hand from his mouth, fingers covered in blood (a dark pool of it in his palm, the viscous liquid dripping thickly to the floor), Illiaz reached out.

At first Lux thought Illiaz was reaching for him, and was about to decide to step forward, step back, or remain where he was; but after a moment, it became clear that Illiaz wasn't reaching for him. His delicate white spider-mum fingers purposefully smeared blood over the floor. He was concentrating with everything he had, writing upside down and backwards so Lux could read it easily.

Please don't go, the blood scrawled over the black and white tiles, and Lux wondered where he would go. Except for forward. There was nowhere he could go except for forward.

He took a step, but he suddenly felt overwhelmingly queasy. His legs buckled and brought him to his hands and knees, his stomach heaving violently and painfully as he vomited.

When the heaving stopped and his stomach calmed enough for him to raise a hand from the mess and wipe his mouth, he saw the contents of his stomach emptied out on the floor.

He went still, eyes widening.

There were dismembered fingers in his stomach acid. Toes.

Someone's heart. It gave one last beat, then went still.

Lux pressed a hand to his chest; his heart beat reassuringly against his ribs. It wasn't his own heart on the floor in front of him.

He looked up at Illiaz, who had that gaping hole through his chest, and Lux wondered suddenly if the heart was Illiaz's—but as soon as he looked up, he went still again. Illiaz was a corpse on the floor, swarmed with glistening black skin beetles. They were crawling over him, eating him, squirming out of his ears, his eye sockets, between his bloodless lips.

Lux could only stare, feeling his heartbeat rise and then slow again. He wished, somewhere far off in the beyond-the-horizon distance of his mind, that he could get away. The echoes of the thought faded with the solidity of the realization that he couldn't.

There was no point in trying to turn and run in the opposite direction when this was what was in front of him. There would be no getting away from this.

Illiaz had been all he'd had in the world.

The skin beetles, turning away from Illiaz's corpse, were crawling toward him. They reached him, and he couldn't pull away. They scuttled over his skin, over his body and face, into his mouth. He jerked violently as he tried desperately to spit them out—

And slammed his head into Illiaz's.

"Ow!" Illiaz gave an involuntary yelp, touching his forehead and wincing.

The pain in Lux's own head quickly dissipated. He looked at Illiaz in the dark, noting that he was whole, alive, and smelling only faintly of blood beneath the rose and sandalwood of his cologne. "Sorry. I didn't realize you were leaning over me when I sat up like that."

Illiaz snorted slightly, looking at him with dilated eyes from between his pale fingers. "Another bad dream?"

Lux tilted his head. "'Another'?"

Illiaz closed his eyes and exhaled slowly, lowering his hand. He asked, "You still don't remember that you get them most nights?"

Lux thought that they'd been sleeping during the days more often than during the nights, but he just held Illiaz's gaze for a long moment. There was nothing readable there, and he looked away, down at the damask embroidery of the duvet. "...I hope I don't scream too loudly."

Illiaz shook his head. "You've never screamed," he said. It was utterly assured, the way he stated it.

Lux glanced at him. "I see."

Except that he didn't, because he didn't remember anything.

"Stay out of the sunlight, Lux," Illiaz had told him.

He kept forgetting.

HIS NAME WAS Luxanthus Nkidu Madubabakar. He'd been the Second Prince of the desert kingdom of Ordyuk, called a Blessed warrior, and now he was a gladiator in the kingdom of Mythus's Arena, in which fighters and accursed monsters fought each other to the death.

One of the Monster Killers was a warrior they all called Mimic because he had the word carved in large letters over his chest and back. It looked like the wound had been quite painful when it had been inflicted, but Mimic always fought bare-chested, openly displaying the scars. He had pale skin, and the scar was dark with a reddish tone at the edges that was almost the same shade as his softly red hair and red-gold eyes.

Mimic's signature fighting style was mimicking the movements of anyone he saw after seeing them only once. He picked up new moves in the middle of battles and used them against his opponents.

For some reason, however, he couldn't copy Luxanthus's fighting style. Or rather, he could copy the moves themselves, but he couldn't get the rhythm, and his attempts looked stilted and caused him to be off-balance.

Mimic was generally almost absurdly bright and cheerful, but something about Luxanthus rattled him. He kept blithely insisting on fighting Luxanthus, but each time he did, he grew more and more frustrated and distraught.

"Again," he'd say, and Luxanthus would acquiesce.

Finally, after one fight, Mimic had his hands on his knees, sweat dripping down over the word carved into his chest and back. He looked up at Luxanthus with a despairing expression and said, "What's going on in your mind as you're fighting?"

"Nothing in particular," Luxanthus said, wiping away his own sweat. "It's not like I'm thinking about what I'm doing. I'm just reacting." He'd rehearsed his drills again and again, until he could do them backward and forward with his eyes closed. He honestly wouldn't have been surprised if he'd been told he even did them in his sleep.

Something dawned in Mimic's face.

"Again," he said, straightening.

This time, as the two of them fought, Mimic's eyes had gone completely lifeless.

After that fight, Luxanthus had gotten shivers.

It really had been just like he would've imagined fighting himself to be.

"I guess you're not a Blessed warrior, after all," Mimic told him later, a grin curling his lips. He was back to his usual animated self. "If you were, it wouldn't be possible for me to mimic you."

"What am I, then?" Luxanthus asked him, subdued.

Mimic laughed and shook his head. "You just have an unusual mindset. Really hard to get into, and not all that fun." He shrugged and said, "I'd assess it as being good for fighting, but not for much else."

Luxanthus couldn't help but smile wryly. "I agree with that assessment."

Mimic patted him on the arm and said, "You're really not that bad, Luxanthus. You're just cursed with an utter insensitivity to fear. That's what makes you so difficult for everyone."

He walked away humming and rubbing the scar on his chest,

and Luxanthus looked after him, thinking.

ILLIAZ WAS LOOKING at Lux discerningly, the whites of his eyes seeming to glow slightly in the dark. "Did you remember something from your dream, this time?"

"No…" Lux didn't think that what he'd seen had anything to do with memories. Lying back on the bed, he looked at the dark stone ceiling. "When we fall asleep, where do we go?"

Illiaz lay down next to him, staring upward as well, hands tucked behind his head. "Into our minds, I suppose," he answered. "Where else?"

Lux ran his tongue over the sharp edges of his teeth. "So if I keep having bad dreams, what does that say about what's inside my mind?"

Illiaz rolled onto his side to face him, looking at him in the dark. "That it's frightening or disturbing in some way, I would take it," he said easily, and Lux could make out the trace of a smile on his lips.

"And that doesn't scare you?"

"No."

Lux sat up, looking down at him. "What do you know?"

Illiaz remained lying there on his side, smiling. "That you're not an intentionally cruel person, Lux."

Lux had the urge to smother Illiaz with a pillow. Or perhaps simply with his hand. He closed his eyes.

"So you're certain that I won't kill you?"

"No," Illiaz said. "I'm certain that if you do, it means I deserved it." He laughed, jubilant.

Lux felt his own lips quirking. "Heh." He straightened his head so that his eyes were staring through his closed eyelids at a memory of the stone ceiling. "I think I might actually like you."

He knew that Illiaz was smiling. "Everyone does."

Lux huffed slightly. "What an opinion you have of yourself." He opened his eyes, staring up toward the ceiling swathed in the dense shadows above him. "What is it that you actually want from me, Illiaz?"

Illiaz was silent for several moments. The quiet was filled with the distant pattering of rain on the balcony beyond the closed doors. When Illiaz finally answered, it was with a rueful laugh. "...A reason to live, I suppose."

"Without me you don't have one?"

Illiaz blinked his moth-pale eyelashes in the dark. There was childish wonder in his expression. "...You really do ask the most merciless questions," he said, laughing gently. "And you know, I really don't feel like answering that one."

"Sorry."

Illiaz smiled at him in the dark, simultaneously soft and sad and something else: something brighter. "Anyone," he said, "would have memory issues after going through what you've been through."

Lux looked at him silently, and Illiaz looked back at him, equally silent.

Lux let out a sigh. No matter how long he waited, Illiaz would not be elaborating. "You seem determined not to tell me what that was." If his expectant silence wasn't enough to reach the truth, no number of words would get him there.

"You'll remember when you're ready," Illiaz said simply.

"And if I never do?"

"Then it'll be because it's not necessary." A smile blossomed in his voice, the promise of a laugh the way daffodils were a promise of spring. "You've always done whatever's necessary," he remarked, the flowery potential for a laugh fulfilling itself fondly, "but nothing before that."

Lux opened his eyes to look back at him, meeting Illiaz's gaze. "You admire that." Lux curved his lips away from the sharpness of his teeth. "Which means that you yourself are not like that."

"No, I'm not," Illiaz agreed. "I have a tendency to go to unnecessarily excessive lengths."

Lux observed him listlessly. "Because you want things." His lips were caking slightly with drying blood. He licked them clean. "Even if they're not necessary, those things…you want them."

Illiaz held his gaze unflinchingly, and agreed, "Yes."

Lux felt a tug at his moistened lips like the pathetic twitching of a dying arachnid. "I can see why I might've liked you." He chuckled, as scorpions would scuttle. "I imagine I admired that you know what you want and are willing to go to any lengths to obtain it."

"I always had the feeling I rather baffled and disconcerted you," Illiaz admitted.

"You still do."

"That's okay," Illiaz said. "As long as you don't leave…" His hand reached out toward Lux, but hesitated in the darkness of the air, as a snake would in front of a flute.

"Like I did before?" Lux regarded him, tilting his head. "Did you manage to chase me away?"

Somewhere far away were rolling dunes of golden, windswept sand. Lux wondered how he knew that.

"No," Illiaz said, "it wasn't by your intention."

"By mistake?"

"No." Illiaz shook his head. With death's utter certainty, he said, "I doubt you've ever made a mistake in your life."

There was a sting in Lux's mouth, similar to starlight. "Am I human?" He felt light enough to float away, and wondered if he was dreaming or if this was real; if he was who he thought he was or if he was someone else entirely. It was possible, after all, to be someone else in a dream.

But if it was a dream, and he knew it was a dream, that didn't explain why he wasn't waking up. Perhaps that meant it was real. Or perhaps reality was nothing but a dream from which one couldn't awaken.

Lux certainly didn't know. There was very little that he knew.

"Stay out of the sunlight, Lux," Illiaz had told him.

He wondered if entering the sunlight was more like falling asleep or more like waking up.

HIS NAME WAS Luxanthus Nkidu Madubabakar. He'd been the Second Prince of the desert kingdom of Ordyuk, called a Blessed warrior, and now he was a gladiator in the kingdom of Mythus's Arena, in which fighters and accursed monsters fought each other to the death.

The other Monster Killer from Hahsin was called Kayds. His most distinctive feature was his hair, which was black on his right side and white on his left, making his gray eyes appear to be two different shades. He was also the shortest of the Monster Killers and the slightest of figure. He was covered in brutal-looking scars. He loved fighting more than any of them, and he didn't shy away from pain.

Fighting with Kayds, Luxanthus had to try his utmost *not* to accidentally kill him. And it was obvious Kayds realized this, because he would throw himself in the way of Luxanthus's weapon in order to get him to pull back his blow, which the Hahsinian warrior would then use to press his advantage. If Luxanthus hadn't defended himself, Kayds would have killed him; that was how seriously Kayds was attacking.

"You're fighting like you don't want to hurt me," Kayds accused as they sparred.

"I don't," Luxanthus affirmed, staying on the defensive.

"It's not any fun if you fight like that," Kayds snapped at him, bringing his scythe down hard against the blunt club that Luxanthus had chosen as his weapon. *"Hurt me!"* Undoubtedly due to his short figure and limited reach, Kayds preferred long weapons, particularly the spear and the scythe. He was adept with both.

Luxanthus had learned to fight him with a club so that he could hit him without killing him.

When he hit Kayds with rib-cracking force, the Hahsinian warrior laughed in delight. *"That's* more like it!" Kayds rushed back in with renewed fervor.

Luxanthus wondered what it was about the Hahsin training that produced warriors who *liked* pain.

"By the deities' curses, you've got a really boring expression on your face," Kayds told him as they fought.

"So I've been told," Luxanthus replied dryly, parrying Kayds's blows easily.

When Kayds suddenly stopped fighting, lowering all his defenses, Luxanthus pulled up short.

Kayds used the opening to slash his scythe at him, actually managing to graze Luxanthus's side. Luxanthus, having sprung out of the way at the last moment, was astonished.

He couldn't remember the last time anyone had managed to hit him.

Kayds was looking at him with his light and dark eyes.

"Curses," he sighed, tossing his scythe aside in disappointment. "Your expression is still boring. This is no fun." He left the training arena.

He never asked Luxanthus to spar again.

Luxanthus, later, would find himself wondering why that fact stung.

It wasn't his fault that he was this way. Blessed, cursed, or whatever he was.

ILLIAZ WAS LOOKING at him with an unreadable expression. He said nothing, and yet Lux had the sudden urge to cover his ears.

Sometimes silence rang louder than words.

"Am I not human?" Lux smiled after he asked it, feeling abruptly that this was all rather amusing. Ridiculous, even. Absurd, meaningless, and yet all there was in the world. "All humans make mistakes, do they not? I feel like I remember that fact." He didn't know how he knew that somewhere far away there were rolling dunes of golden sand being shifted by the wind.

Illiaz looked at him, curved his lips, and shook his head as a dog would. Lux knew what a dog was but didn't know how he knew. In his mind, though, were sharp teeth, yellow eyes, panting tongues, and a fluid motion of limbs. Maybe it was the memory of a dog. Or perhaps it was simply reflections he'd caught of himself.

Illiaz was still smiling at him. Even in the darkness—with his eyes fully dilated, his irises swallowed by his black pupils—Lux felt that Illiaz's eyes were blue. "Your mind, I swear..." Illiaz said. The smile broke away from him into the air in the form of a laugh, filling the room like fireflies. "You're going to be the death of me."

It was dark in the room, yet Illiaz's smile was bright and unwavering no matter how closely Lux examined it.

Lux realized he could hear the distant singing of birds. When he looked to the curtains shrouding the windows, there were dim smudges of rose-gray sunlight at the edges. "...It's sunny outside, isn't it?" He looked back to Illiaz, who was pale and nearly insubstantial in the deep shadow of the room. "Why do you tell me not to go into the sun?" He wondered, sometimes. When he remembered to.

Illiaz simply shrugged again. "Well, you could try going outside into the sun, but you probably wouldn't get very far...." He gestured with his skeletal hand and said, "You can open the curtain and see, if you want." He was phlegmatic bordering on lethargic, meeting Lux's eyes in the dark and smiling without feeling. "If you want to, I won't stop you."

Lux's mouth felt dry, and his limbs felt heavy. "...I don't think I really care." He looked away from the heavy curtains with the sunlight creeping jaundiced at their edges and again met Illiaz's dark gaze. "I'll just trust you."

Illiaz looked at him blankly for a moment; then a grin blossomed on his face. A moment later it had unfurled into a laugh. "That's very like you," he said.

Lux looked back at him for a moment, then looked away again, exhaling softly. "I wouldn't know."

Maybe if he went out into the sun, it would be warm on his skin. But maybe it would scorch him behind his eyes.

HIS NAME WAS Luxanthus Nkidu Madubabakar. He'd been the Second Prince of the desert kingdom of Ordyuk, called a Blessed warrior, and now he was a gladiator in the kingdom of Mythus's Arena, in which fighters and accursed monsters fought each other to the death.

Among the Monster Killers were a pair of brothers named Ontarion and Regerius.

They didn't look very much alike. Ontarion was slighter in build and had short white-blond hair and fulvous-red eyes; Regerius was taller and broader, with a blue eye and long golden-blond hair. One could tell they were brothers only by how close they were.

Technically, only Ontarion was one of the Monster Killers; Regerius, despite living in the same barracks, did not fight, as he was missing both his right eye and his right arm. By the way he still winced when he moved, it was clear that the wounds weren't yet fully healed.

"What happened?" Luxanthus asked him.

"It got cut off," Regerius said dryly. Referring, it seemed, only to his arm.

"Okay," Luxanthus said. He certainly couldn't make Regerius tell him if he didn't want to. Although he was able to infer, since Regerius had said 'cut' rather than 'ripped' or 'torn,' that it had been the work of a human rather than of a monster.

Regerius regarded him with his single blue eye narrowed, clearly wondering if Luxanthus was going to ask anything else. Luxanthus didn't; he wasn't particularly interested. He wondered only idly, watching Regerius roll his shoulder and wince, what could have removed his arm and eye without damaging any of the rest of him.

When Ontarion walked in and saw them together, he hissed at Luxanthus and pulled Regerius protectively to his side.

Ah, so it had probably been one of the other gladiators. Lucky him, to still be alive.

It was also strangely merciful of the guards to let Regerius live there when only his brother was able to fight. But Luxanthus supposed that Ontarion was good enough at slaying the Accursed to make it worth housing and feeding them both. He was a fast and brutal close-range fighter, preferring short weapons and aiming straight for the throat and eyes. He didn't dance around or toy with his opponents; he went straight for the kill. Unlike some of the others, he didn't seem to enjoy fighting. He only ever smiled when he was with Regerius.

The two of them were exceptionally close. Outside of the Arena, they were always together, touching each other, sharing smiles, or whispering into each other's ears. They seemed happy.

Seeing how close they were, Luxanthus couldn't help but think that he had never been that close with any of his siblings. Not even his younger brother, Tmra, who'd become a Blessed warrior and had fought at his side with feathered arms, scales on his body, and fingers that could disintegrate anything he touched. They'd gotten along quite well, once Tmra had been able to keep pace with him.

But they'd never been as close as Ontarion and Regerius. Luxanthus didn't think he'd ever been all that close with anyone.

ILLIAZ, ON THE BED beside Lux, was curled in on himself, clutching his stomach and shaking uncontrollably. The taste of blood in Lux's mouth when he bit at his lower lip was like a spark. His head felt empty like a carved-out gourd. "...Do you need a glass of water?"

Illiaz made a choking sound, a hand flying to his mouth as his eyes widened. He then managed to, somehow, fall off the bed and collapse to the ground in a fit of raucous laughter. Lux wasn't quite sure how he'd done it.

Lux rolled over to stare down at Illiaz on the floor. Illiaz was laughing so hard that he looked as if he were being racked by pain. The sound was gasping, and he had one arm around his stomach while the other was clamped over his mouth. Laughter was leaking through his fingers, though. Dark like blood.

Illiaz hadn't said yes to the glass of water, and Lux didn't know what to do, so he just lay there on the bed and watched. He didn't understand why Illiaz was laughing, but it didn't matter; he didn't particularly care. He wondered only idly, watching Illiaz tremble and hack up laughter like blood through his fingers, what could possibly have been so funny about what he'd said.

The dizzying scent of blood filling the room from Lux's cut lip had his head spinning.

A concave emptiness opened in Lux's stomach, making him cold. It was leaking in air through his mouth, so he stuffed his hand into the space, as far back as it would go.

The next thing he knew, the world started shaking, and his hand was torn from his mouth. "Lux! Lux, stop! Stop it!"

Lux blinked and saw Illiaz standing over him, eyes the blue of soft azurite, skin and hair all soft gypsum. Lux had the feeling that if he reached up to touch him, Illiaz would crumble like chalk. "What?" There was blood in his mouth, and he blinked again.

He became aware that his hand was being clenched, Illiaz's pale and delicate fingers between his darker, muscled ones, which were dripping with blood. The dark red covered his skin as if he'd been crushing dark cherries in his fist.

"You…" Illiaz started. He looked away, tightening his grip around Lux's bloodied fingers. "…had a nightmare. Again. You were biting your hand."

"Oh." That explained the pain. Lux watched the way Illiaz wouldn't meet his gaze and realized the way that he'd said 'again' meant that this kind of thing had happened before, and that Illiaz probably didn't realize that Lux didn't remember it.

"I'm sorry." He didn't know what was wrong with him, and Illiaz wasn't telling him. Or maybe he'd told before, but Lux had forgotten. Maybe Illiaz had eventually stopped telling him since he was just going to keep forgetting, anyway.

Lux didn't know how long he'd been in this mansion, and he didn't know at what point the dreams that had been doggedly but distantly following him finally had caught up with him; but catch up with him they had. And in catching up to him, they had sunk their teeth into him and begun tearing pieces of his mind away, till he wasn't sure what was real and what wasn't.

Illiaz was looking at him, smiling sadly, the expression all close-mouthed snapdragon. "It's not your fault..."

The blood was dripping down Lux's arm, but it wasn't just his arm—his chest was smeared with it, and so was the bed. He looked back at Illiaz. "Did I do this?" There were flecks of blood even on Illiaz's cheek, although he had clearly just bathed—smelling of rose-and-sandalwood soap, with his hair dripping water down onto Lux's face.

The smile Illiaz gave became a curling, elaborate spider chrysanthemum. "Well," he said, shrugging with enough airiness to challenge that of a teasing breeze, *"I* didn't do it." He was still holding on to Lux's hand, and his wet hair dripped water continuously onto Lux's face, the drops tickling first and then itching second.

Lux's other sleeve was clean, and he wrapped the fabric around his unbloodied hand and reached up with it to squeeze the water from Illiaz's dripping bangs. "I'm sorry."

Illiaz shook his head, shedding more droplets of water onto Lux's skin. "Like I said, it's not your fault," he repeated, and stepped back, pulling Lux up from the bloodied duvet with the slightest of gestures. "Don't worry." He let go of Lux's hand and pushed him gently. "I'll clean it."

Lux took a step, then stopped. There was a lot more spilled blood than he'd realized. He felt distantly guilty. "I can help."

Illiaz waved a hand flippantly. "Don't worry about it. I'd prefer to do it myself." He made a shooing motion, gesturing for Lux to head to the bathroom. With an almost disconcerting amount of force, he said, "You go clean yourself."

Lux's mouth still tasted sweetly, saltily, bitterly of blood. "I'm sorry."

Illiaz shook his head, his lips quirking. The expression was gentle, diffident, like the hanging of bluebells. "No, no, it's not that," he said, with a minute shake of his head. "It's that nobody else can ever clean anything to my satisfaction." He laughed, then: soft stirrings as from butterfly wingbeats. "It's a lot easier to just clean things myself." Butterflies fluttering erratically in the air, dazzling glances of bright colors that, at any moment, might crumple and fall.

Lux watched Illiaz try to hold up the graceful strokes of his smile in the flickering of the candlelight and felt a sliding and a slotting in his mind, as of disassembled images falling into place, weaving together with jittery skitterings. "...There have been spiderwebs in the mansion, recently."

Spiderwebs at the ceilings and in the corners, where he was now becoming certain they hadn't used to be. He thought he remembered once, some time ago, wondering at the fact that the mansion, despite being large and seemingly near-empty of inhabitants, was impeccably well-kept and clean, without dust or cobwebs. He thought he remembered, more recently, staring up at an elaborate spiderweb—its creator hanging long- and many-legged at its center—and wondering at how such a small being was able to create something that complex and sublime.

"...I must have missed those," Illiaz said stiltedly, his gaze averted while his voice and smile cracked.

Lux blinked at him. "It doesn't bother me." Something about spiders and spiderwebs reminded him of deities; of sunlight shining hot on shifting desert sands.

When Illiaz met his gaze, it was as from deep shadow. "No," he agreed, "I imagine it wouldn't."

Lux felt that he was watching someone trying to make a statue of themselves by holding perfectly, artfully still, with every angle and line of their form carefully and intentionally positioned just so. "Does it bother you that much?"

Illiaz shrugged, lightly but with a sense of weight. As if the atrophied muscles of his back were pulled taut by the presence of wings—as of those pallid and skeletal beings that populated the manor's murals along with the insect-legged monsters from Lux's dreams. An abundance of things in the mansion that did not make sense.

Lux's blood-moist tongue darted over his thirst-cracked lips. "The suits of armor in the halls are also damaged. And the statues along the stairwells are missing their heads." He regarded the refined sculpture of Illiaz's carefully held form. "That doesn't bother you?"

Illiaz laughed softly. "They're clean, aren't they?" He smiled wryly. "I don't mind if things are broken—it's only when things are dirty that I'm bothered." He was still laughing, seemingly to himself. Or perhaps at himself.

The disconnected pieces in Lux's head splintered, breaking and then threading themselves delicately but surely together. "Then you don't mind that I keep having nightmares." It hadn't made any sense that Illiaz wasn't scared of him. "Just the blood that gets everywhere." Now it did.

Illiaz had doubled over with his laughter, which was again too rampageous for his feeble form. Now, he righted himself with an elegant brush of a hand back through his bangs. "I suppose so." His bangs fell back into his face, over his right eye. His left was still shining, but its gaze was catching on the blood on Lux's hand, his chest, the bed, and the floor.

Following Illiaz's gaze, Lux tilted his head. "How did I manage to do that, anyway?" He lifted his hand, turning it this way and that in the candlelight as he regarded the blood congealing over his unblemished flesh. "Where did all the blood come from, if my skin isn't broken?" He looked at Illiaz past the silhouette of his bloody hand. "Are you…sure it's mine?"

Illiaz snorted, immediately disparaging. "Well, it's not mine, and it's not anyone else's." Exasperation tinged his voice like night creeping into evening. He turned away and waved a hand. "Go wash yourself while I take care of this."

Lux exhaled, lowering his hand and turning away to step toward the bathroom. He stopped, glancing back. "Do I know other people aside from you?" Illiaz had said the blood didn't only not belong to him, but that it also 'wasn't anybody else's,' which suggested that there were other people whose blood it could be.

Sometimes, Lux forgot that there were other people in the world; then Illiaz would mention them. Somewhere, they existed. The fact seemed utterly irrelevant most of the time. But perhaps it was more relevant than Lux realized.

Illiaz looked at him over his shoulder, the bone of the joint sharp through the loose fabric of his indigo shirt. His black pants were tight only at his waist and ankles, the rest all billowy folds like rose petals, as if to obscure his emaciated form. It made his pale bony feet stand out against the carpet and his pale thin hands look spidery as he gestured, like the skittery creators of the webs that were gathering in the mansion's dark corners.

"I don't know if you remember anyone else now, but you certainly knew others at one point." Illiaz's dark shirt shimmered, the play of the light and shadows further hiding whatever bones were pressing through the skin beneath the loose silk. "I'm not the only person in the world."

Lux felt like he was forgetting something. "At the moment, you seem to be." He found himself curious only about what it was, out of all the things he'd forgotten, that he was vaguely recalling the loss of.

It was as if the sun, instead of shining ahead of him and lighting his way, had fallen behind him, casting his shadow such that he was walking into its darkness. He couldn't see where he was stepping, and whenever he turned to look behind him, there was nothing of his presence there. All of his memory evaporated by the sun's blinding light.

"Stay out of the sunlight, Lux," Illiaz had told him.

He wondered how many times he had forgotten.

HIS NAME WAS Luxanthus Nkidu Madubabakar. He'd been the Second Prince of the desert kingdom of Ordyuk, called a Blessed warrior, and now he was a gladiator in the kingdom of Mythus's Arena, in which fighters and accursed monsters fought each other to the death. He was very, very good at killing the Accursed, and he was housed in the barracks with others who were like him.

That was, until one day he was moved out of the barracks to stay in the Fonhellansicht manor, at the request of Illiaz Fonhellansicht.

Luxanthus went, simply because it was required of him. He didn't think living there would be any different, except that Tiyrrin wouldn't be shying away from him, Jyunpey wouldn't be trying to get under his skin, Velurid wouldn't be begging him to hurt him, Aiyler wouldn't be wincing every time he appeared, Renz wouldn't be angrily demanding to fight him, Mimic wouldn't be fighting him with utterly dead eyes, and Ontarion wouldn't be hissing at him and pulling Regerius away.

When he first met Illiaz, Illiaz smiled at him like Luxanthus was the sun. There was nothing behind the flame-blue of his eyes aside from unadulterated wonder and delight. "You're an incredible fighter, Luxanthus."

Nobody had smiled at Luxanthus like that since his little brother, Tmra, had grown into himself and stopped watching his training. Luxanthus had forgotten what it felt like: being looked at as if he had the power to make the entire world brighter.

He'd missed it, he realized.

He'd missed it a lot.

It was nice to be more than just a harbinger of death.

"Do you mind if I call you Lux?"

Luxanthus had never been able to say no to that kind of smile. "That's fine."

It was why he'd always fought monsters, after all—so that people would smile at him like that. As if he were Blessed.

ILLIAZ WAS LOOKING at him, though Lux didn't notice until Illiaz disrupted his thoughts with an uneven breath.

Lux glanced back at him. The quality of the light in Illiaz's eyes and the tilt of his lips were indecipherable.

Illiaz asked, "...Is that selfish of me?"

Lux blinked uncomprehendingly. "Is what selfish of you?" He felt that he'd missed something, somewhere. Or maybe he'd just forgotten. It was as if the spiderweb-threads with which he had woven together the disconnected pieces in his mind kept disintegrating, burned away by the sunlight of *now;* torn apart in the wind of passing time. Lux found sense and meaning for a moment, then lost both again.

Illiaz said, "That I seem to be the only person in your world."

Lux blinked at him once more. "That you...?" Again, the spiderwebs had disintegrated. Lux glanced up at the ceiling as for something to direct his thoughts—a helpful spider hiding in a corner, perhaps—but all he found was darkness.

Well, that was all there was anywhere for him. "It's my world we're talking about, isn't it?" He glanced over at Illiaz, lips curving wryly. "If you seem to be the only person in my world, then that's my fault, not yours—because it's my world and not yours."

He'd already forgotten what they'd been talking about. If it were important, the memory would stay, or would at least turn up again.

"And?" Illiaz was exceedingly icy and pale, as if he were meant to have sunlight glancing off him. Yet he was there in the dark with the candlelight flickering tongues over his skin. The bruise-black and sleepless-purple blooms of his clothes swallowed him like dark swells.

Well, everything disappeared eventually, especially in Lux's mind. "I don't know."

His body was made of stone, but his mind was wisps of fog. Maybe he was a mountain. Stretched between the earth and the clouds, high and far apart such that he couldn't see from one end of himself to the other.

He didn't know what he was thinking.

Illiaz's voice brought him back down from the blurry-distant height with a longsuffering sigh of, "Go clean yourself." There was blood dripping from the corner of Illiaz's mouth.

Lux glanced at him. "And you?"

"What?"

Lux, with his blood-darkened hand, gestured to the blood that was darkening Illiaz's lips. "You've got blood on you, too."

Illiaz's eyes widened, and his hand flew to his mouth. His gaze averted while his body went rigid. "..." He coughed slightly, the sound rasping and wet.

Lux watched him. "You're bleeding."

Illiaz wouldn't look at him. Something dark and void-cold curled in Lux's chest.

"Did I do that?"

Illiaz shook his head quickly. "No," he murmured from behind his fingers.

Lux watched as Illiaz reached into the folds of his loose pants and pulled out a dark handkerchief, pressed it to his mouth. Lux's tongue ran over his lips. His hand was itching where the blood was drying on his skin. "...You wouldn't lie to me about that, would you?"

Illiaz shook his head again, dark handkerchief over the lower half of his face. "No." He pulled the cloth away just enough so his voice wouldn't be muffled. "It's fine." His posture was rigid.

Lux watched him for another moment, then turned away. He exhaled slowly, darkly, emptily. "Well, you're not going to tell me anything that you don't want me to know." He brought his itching hand to his chest and started scratching. "Go ahead and carry whatever burden you feel like carrying." Looking at the gold bangle around his wrist, he let out a snort. "If you don't want to weigh me down with whatever knowledge you're keeping to yourself, you can weigh me down with gold."

There was a metal bangle around his other wrist, too, and

around his ankles, bands to which the chains attached. Lux glanced over at where they were laid out on the bedside table. "I suppose there are the chains, as well." Not that any of it was very heavy.

Illiaz looked at him, and then away again, the dark handkerchief still pressed carefully over his mouth. "I'm sorry," he said, muffled-quiet from behind it.

Lux waved a hand, gold bangle brushing quietly against the muscled flesh of his wrist. "It's fine. It doesn't bother me any."

"Which part?" Illiaz asked carefully.

Lux shrugged, dried blood cracking itchingly over his skin. "All of it; none of it bothers me." If there were any reasons for him to care, then Illiaz was keeping those from him, too.

He regarded Illiaz's still form. "I don't know if it's because I don't remember anything, but I don't really feel anything." Nothing but emptiness—which was a feeling as much as fullness was. Between the two, Lux figured it was better to feel hungry than to feel glutted.

Illiaz let out a short exhale through his nose. "No." He pulled the dark handkerchief away from his face and glanced down at it, his lips curving slightly. "You've always been like that." The bleeding seemed to have stopped, his lips clean.

"So you knew?"

Illiaz met his gaze with eyes like hollow night skies with distant stars shining. "I've always known," Illiaz said, with his mouth curling up into a darkness-flowering smile.

In Lux's mind, spiders skittered over their webs, carefully weaving. "You care for me despite that?" The edges of his teeth were sharp scraping over the tip of his tongue. "Or because of it?"

Illiaz's gaze was too sultry, too warm. "Both." He smiled, all curling, unfurling thin petals of spider chrysanthemum. "Go wash yourself already."

Lux blinked. "Right. I forgot." He glanced up at the ceiling for a moment, then at Illiaz again, finding his lips twitching slightly. Dry like flowers gone dead. "Maybe not for the first time, huh."

Illiaz's smile was fresh supple petals, fragrant and darkly blooming. "You claim not to care about anything," he said, almost mocking, "but you're always asking questions."

Lux blinked at him again, then turned his gaze away. The ceiling was dark. Lux wondered if there were any spiderwebs. "I suppose so. I guess I am still curious. It occurs to me to ask, but then it doesn't occur to me to care when I don't receive answers." He shrugged, lowering his gaze. "Whatever that means. I really don't know anything." He wondered idly if he was getting flakes of dried blood on the elaborate floral rug. Dark brown-red specks on the ivory and mauve.

Illiaz's tone was balmy, sunlit like summer and oppressive like humidity. "Life is funny, huh?"

Lux didn't dare to lift his eyelids enough to raise his dark eyelashes out of his vision. "I wouldn't know."

"No," Illiaz agreed, and laughed, smoke-blurry, "I suppose you wouldn't."

Since Lux apparently forgot everything.

He was certain that he was going to forget this, too.

The candlelight cast the shadows of his eyelashes down his cheeks. The aftertaste of blood in his mouth was starting to make him feel hungry. He glanced down at his hand, where the blood had dried dark red-brown on the brazen tone of his marble skin. "I should go wash myself before I forget again."

"You should," agreed Illiaz, and Lux nodded, turning and heading to the bathroom. He shucked off his shirt and washed away the blood. Then he rinsed off the garment and scrubbed it till the bloodstains didn't show. But then the fabric was wet, so he dropped the garment over the edge of the bath.

"Stay out of the sunlight, Lux," Illiaz had told him.

He wondered what would happen when he forgot.

HIS NAME WAS Luxanthus Nkidu Madubabakar. He'd been the Second Prince of the desert kingdom of Ordyuk, called a Blessed warrior, and now he was a gladiator in the kingdom of Mythus's Arena, in which fighters and accursed monsters fought each other to the death. He'd been housed in the barracks with others like him up until he moved to stay in the Fonhellansicht manor, at the request of Illiaz Fonhellansicht.

Now Luxanthus was training not in the Practice Arena, but in the Fonhellansicht horse corral, the horses all put away and the area cleaned of dung and hay. Now there was just dust and dirt, far more solid than the sand arenas of Ordyuk.

Illiaz was there, seated on the edge of the fence, watching him. "Lux," he said, a curious tilt to his head.

Luxanthus paused in his exercises to look at him. "Yes?"

Illiaz's smile lingered. "Thank you," he said.

Luxanthus blinked at him, confused. "For what?"

"For indulging me," Illiaz said, lips softly curled. But it wasn't like Luxanthus had a choice.

"Sure," he said.

Illiaz hummed. "For what reason do you wear all that gold?" he asked, a curious light in his flame-blue eyes.

Luxanthus inhaled, exhaled again. "...It's too easy, otherwise," he admitted, not without reservation. He'd tried to cover himself with jewelry so that he wouldn't win so effortlessly, but the fact that he still won despite the handicap made the others hate him all the more.

But Illiaz just looked at him and asked, "What is?"

"Defeating the Accursed," Luxanthus said. "I thought, if I weighed myself down, it might be more of a challenge. If it were more challenging, it might be a little more fun." Most of the others had looked like they'd enjoyed fighting the Accursed in the Arena.

Luxanthus couldn't remember if fighting had ever been fun for him. What was it that made Jyunpey, Renz, and Kayds grin with such delight as they hurt others or were hurt themselves? What was it that made Tiyrrin, Velurid, and Ontarion so content after their victories? Why was it that Mimic, when he was copying the others' fighting styles, smiled, but when he was copying Luxanthus's style, remained utterly blank?

The audience, after Luxanthus's every victory, cheered and showered him with gold. And yet he still felt hollow.

"And?" Illiaz asked him, appearing nothing but interested. "Does wearing the gold help?"

Luxanthus shrugged. "It makes it slightly harder, but it still doesn't even the scales. It still doesn't make it enjoyable."

"You don't enjoy fighting?"

"It's easy for me," Luxanthus told him. There was a sinking sensation in his stomach. Everyone who knew him had hated him for that ease and been hurt because of it—his siblings; the other gladiators; the monsters. "I don't mind fighting. It's too easy to be particularly engaging, but it's not unpleasant. Battle just feels natural. It feels right." Except when sometimes it was so easy it felt wrong.

Luxanthus couldn't help the sinking of his tone. "I'm just a weapon." He wasn't really human, was he? Not Blessed, but something closer to monstrous or divine than to human.

But Illiaz kept smiling at him. "I think I can understand that," he said. Illiaz kicked his legs slightly, making his light pants shimmer. "After all, I'm just an ornament." He gave a laugh, soft and light like bells. "It's an empty existence, isn't it?"

Luxanthus's bangs fell into his face when he tilted his head. "Is it an empty existence to have a purpose and successfully serve it?"

Illiaz blinked at him, opening his mouth and then closing it again. "When you put it like that," he mused, confusion in his tone and a crinkle between his brows, "it does sound like it should be fulfilling."

Illiaz wore his smile like he wore his makeup and the loose, shimmering silks: like he was covering something up. "So why does it feel hollow?"

Luxanthus's feet were covered in dust. He'd have tan and dirt lines from the sandals when he removed them. "I can't answer that for you."

He just did what was needed of him. No matter how hollow he felt or how much people hated him for being exceptional at what he did, he did what he had to. He fulfilled his purpose.

Illiaz was smiling, but his eyes were glimmering, and he was blinking too fast. "Am I an ornament to you, Lux?" he asked.

Luxanthus shook his head. "You're not," he said.

Illiaz may have dressed elegantly and lined his eyes with colored kohl, but he was primarily Luxanthus's conversation partner.

Almost uncertainly, Luxanthus inquired, "And I'm not just a weapon to you, am I?"

Illiaz shook his head and said, "No, you're not."

Luxanthus felt himself relax slightly. That's what he'd thought.

He didn't know what he and Illiaz were to one another, but whatever it was, it felt different. As if there were fewer expectations. Nothing that he had to fulfill, but also nothing that he could fail.

Perhaps, with each other, they were just two humans, neither Blessed nor cursed.

LUX LEFT HIS wet shirt in the bathroom and came out to find woven baskets full of gold jewelry on the floor.

Illiaz had removed the bloody duvet and was smoothing a clean one over the bed. Lux looked from the large piles of gold jewelry over to him. "...Are you sure you don't have any more gold?" There was quite a lot. Far more than he'd expected. He didn't know that he'd actually been expecting anything. He'd been mostly joking when he'd asked. He'd then almost entirely forgotten his joke.

Illiaz snorted, brushing out the crinkles in the satin fabric. "You asked for it," he pointed out. "Didn't you say you wanted to be weighed down?"

Lux's lips twitched. "So I did." He knelt and tipped over the woven baskets to spread the jewelry out over the floor. There really was a lot.

He began donning the jewelry piece by piece until he was wearing all of it.

There were enough bangles to go from his wrists to his elbows; enough armbands for him to wear multiple around each bicep; enough anklets to make his every step shimmer and clink; enough rings to wear several on each of his ten fingers. There were collar-pieces from simple chainlike adornments to wide, lavishly orna-mented articles that extended across the shoulders, large and elabo-rate enough to necessitate counterweights in the back. There was a pectoral, with its large lapis lazuli pendant hanging on a gold chain. There was a girdle, gold mesh adorned with stones, which he secured around his waist over his linen sash. There was even a pair of dangling gold earrings, which slid easily through holes in the lobes of his ears that he hadn't realized were there.

Once he'd donned it all, Lux gave a few experimental jumps, arms raised bent at his sides as he tucked his legs to his chest in the air. He gave a few kicks, striking at nothing. A few flat-palmed strikes with his hands. He flipped backward and then forward, did a few handsprings and aerials. It felt as mindless as breathing. As natural as dreaming while sleeping. The gold seemed to draw energy and restlessness from under his skin.

When he was done, he looked over at Illiaz. "It's terribly light." He felt almost disappointed.

Illiaz shook his head and exhaled through his nose as if exas-perated, but his smile was all gentle lotus. "Whether something is light or heavy doesn't say anything about any inherent quality of that thing, but about one's ability to carry it."

Lux blinked. "I suppose that's true." He looked at Illiaz, easily raising his gold-bangled arms and spreading his gold-ringed hands, palms upward. "Then I am clearly capable of carrying more than you're giving me."

Something in Illiaz's blue eyes flickered like flames. "You are," he said. "If I gave you the entire world, I'm sure you'd be able to carry it." His smile was bright but darkening with blood at the corners. "Still, I'm selfish, Lux, and I want to keep some things for my own." He wiped his mouth with the back of a hand, looked down at the dark red smeared over his skin, and smiled like tangled briar: soft petals that danced in the sunlit breezes and sharp thorns that tore deep into skin. "For as long as I can."

His laughter splattered dark behind his fingers and filled the air with the savory scent of blood. Lux's eyes watered slightly. His mouth watered more. He swallowed saliva, looking at Illiaz through lashes heavier than the gold. "Is it your happiness that hurts, or your pain that makes you happy?"

In the darkness Illiaz looked at him, from a pale face, behind pale hair. "Pardon me?" The dark handkerchief was again hiding his mouth.

Lux gestured, his gold bangles clinking against each other quietly. "When you laugh. You're both happy and in pain."

Illiaz's eyelids lowered slightly over his shadowed eyes. His lashes, white as living jasmine, made his skin look a deathly, ashen gray.

When he removed the dark cloth from his mouth there was a smile drying on his lips with the blood. "Should those two things be mutually exclusive?"

There was something in Lux's stomach like snakes. "I suppose not."

Illiaz shook his head. "It's not a matter of one causing the other, Lux," he said, bangs cascaded into his face, white like snow and flurrying with his breaths. His fingers wrapped around the dark handkerchief like pale spiders. "It's not that simple. The pain and the happiness are their own things, existing separately from each other—and yet they're one and the same, utterly inextricable." He shook his head and laughed, all delicate curving calla lily. "Just another thing I can't explain. Like who and what you are—there are no words or utterances that could suffice." He shook his head and laughed once more, the sound flecked with blood and delicate white flowers like poison hemlock, carrying the scent of death. "They simply don't exist."

The ceiling, when Lux looked up at it, was eternal, lifeless darkness. Illiaz, when Lux looked over at him, was pale, living fragility. Lux wanted to flick him with a finger and watch him crumble to dust.

"The way you're keeping me here—caring for me, indulging me, indulging yourself..." There was the promise of death both behind his teeth and jutting with the bones from beneath Illiaz's skin. "Am I anything more than a pet to you?"

Illiaz's laughter sent Lux memories of stars with their pantheons of constellations; their risings, settings, and circlings in the dark. All of them moved around in the heights except for the North Star, which remained stable at the center of the whirling sky. Absolutely, perfectly still—and yet hopelessly dizzy.

"As if you could possibly be reduced to just that," Illiaz interrupted his vertigo, wry as lightning. "You of all people should know that you're not that."

In Lux's mind were distant memories of sunlight, warm on his skin but scorching him behind his eyes.

HIS NAME WAS Luxanthus Nkidu Madubabakar. He'd been the Second Prince of the desert kingdom of Ordyuk, called a Blessed warrior, and now he was a gladiator in the kingdom of Mythus's Arena, in which fighters and accursed monsters fought each other to the death. He was very, very good at killing the Accursed.

But now the entirety of Mythus was overrun with the monsters, giant arachnoid appendages emerging from their bodies, bloody eyes and sharp teeth in terrible mouths that hungered for human flesh. Even Luxanthus could only be in one place at once.

On top of that, there was Illiaz, who was already coughing up blood.

The Fonhellansicht mansion had been attacked, along with the rest of the city. The two of them had retreated up to the roof, but there were too many Accursed. Luxanthus had pulled Illiaz to him with one arm and then jumped, dragging his blade down the side of the mansion to slow their fall.

He would've survived if he hadn't; Illiaz would not have.

The monsters crawled down the side of the mansion after them.

"You shouldn't bother protecting me," Illiaz told him, coughing blood into his palm. "I'm going to die anyway."

"I'm going to protect you," Luxanthus told him. "Just because you're going to die at some point doesn't mean you have to die now."

Illiaz shook his head. "Protecting someone like me will only slow you down. It will hold you back."

Luxanthus pursed his lips. "But I want to," he said, tone quieting. "I know that, logically speaking, I shouldn't—but I *want* to." He quirked his lips slightly as he asked, "Is that selfish of me?"

Illiaz looked at him with wide blue eyes, exhaled, and said, "Yes. That's very selfish of you."

"It was selfish of you to ask for me to be housed with you," Luxanthus said.

"It was indeed selfish of me," Illiaz agreed.

"We all reap what we sow," Luxanthus said, raising his sword as the Accursed again closed in. "If you didn't want me to care about you, then you shouldn't have pulled me close."

"I'm sorry," Illiaz said behind him, voice faint and cracking.

"Don't be," said Luxanthus. "It made me happy." He kept his gaze on the approaching monsters as he asked, "Do you not feel the same?"

There was a wet exhale behind him, and then Illiaz's voice: "I do, yes."

"There you go," Luxanthus said, grip tightening around the hilts of his swords. "If you die then you die; but I'm not giving your life away, Illiaz—I'm incapable of it. So all I'm asking is for you to let me return the favor of desiring to exist in your company."

"Is it a favor?" Illiaz murmured.

"Is it a curse?" Luxanthus asked. "If that's the case, then let us be cursed together. But if it's a blessing, then let us both be blessed."

LUX COULD ONLY STARE at Illiaz, anchoring his fragile and uncertain reality to him as Illiaz gestured grandly, smiling. He reminded Lux of torrents of pouring rain and whippings of howling wind: he was intangible air and delicate raindrops, but there was so much of his PRESENCE that it became something phenomenal.

"I'm not keeping you here," Illiaz said, "but I'm also not making any effort to get you to leave. It's impossible for me to let you go when you never make any attempt to get away, Lux." Illiaz shook his head. His grin was not weak, but rather the powerfully virulent act of *weakening* which was rot itself. "I can't give you away. I'm incapable of it. If you want your freedom, then you need to be the one to take it."

Sunlight crept around the edges of the curtains and in Lux's head: heavy, hot bronze summertime, absent of wind and ringing with the high-pitched droning of cicadas. It was maddening emptiness, and every footstep over the shiftless sand was so easy that it didn't even feel worth taking.

"Freedom, huh?" Lux looked at Illiaz in the dark, both glowing palely in the shadows and being eaten away by them, the aroma of blood on his breath sweetening the air he exhaled. Lux's smile pulled his lips gently away from the sharpness of his teeth. "If freedom is feeling like one isn't trapped and that one is capable of getting all that one wants...then I feel plenty free here."

Illiaz blinked at him. "You..." He shook his head faintly and let out a shaking, bloody laugh. His every movement and utterance caused him pain, as if just carrying his existence was a far heavier burden than all Lux's adorned gold.

Lux wanted to turn Illiaz's painful existence into a necklace to hang around his neck, to see if it would weigh him down and sink his feet into the ground.

As it was, he felt like he was hovering slightly above the floor, everything about him so light and empty that even his mind and memories kept floating away.

Lux looked down at Illiaz from that place where he was walking on air. "If either of us here is locked in chains, it appears to be you, Illiaz."

It had to be Illiaz. Lux could have left easily, but even Illiaz's laughter was so heavy that it doubled him over and brought him collapsing to his knees, bending him further and further till he fell onto his side, curling in on himself and heaving like he was being kicked repeatedly and viciously in the gut. The blood spurted from his mouth with each hacking, laughing breath.

When the laughter eventually subsided, Illiaz looked up at Lux from where he was curled on the floor, colorless-white hair obscuring the painful flame shade of his blue eyes, the handkerchief held to his mouth to staunch the seeping blood. "I'm sure that's true," he murmured, his bloodied lips all red rose when he smiled. His black and blue clothes, like the darkness, gripped bruisingly around him. "I've never known of an instance where you've been wrong."

Lux snorted, feeling his eyes roll like the sun's arcing trajectory across the sky. "I'm sure there are a lot of things that you don't know of." He gestured pointedly with his arms that were covered in gold. "Does where all the jewelry came from happen to be one of them?"

Illiaz blinked from behind his colorless-white bangs. "That's all yours."

Lux looked down at him, blinking in return from behind bangs that were colorless-dark. "Mine." He'd said it dubiously, but he realized a second later that he really should've expected that answer; the jewelry felt right on his body. On top of that, he'd even asked for it. Somewhere in the nearly inaccessible recesses of his forgotten mind, he must have known that the gold adornments existed and that they were his.

"Indeed," Illiaz said, curled on the floor, gesturing with a pale hand like a dove. "So you're the only one who would know where it all came from."

"I never told you?"

Illiaz's hand fell back down with his arm to curl against his chest, a small smile gracing his bloodstained lips even while his shoulders shrugged weakly. "All you ever said on the subject was that people gave it to you because it was too heavy for them, and they couldn't carry it."

Lux's eyes, which had widened minutely, narrowed again. "What were they paying me for?"

Illiaz shook his head, slowly pushing himself up into a sitting position. "I don't think it was payment," he said. "I think it truly was just gifts."

"...Then what were they giving me gifts for?"

Illiaz looked away, pale fingers tensing against the floor, bending like the legs of scorpions. "...And if I tell you that I can't tell you that? That it's too complicated for me to explain without getting into a great many other complicated things?" Illiaz shook his head, gaze down. His lips, darkened by blood, were still visible. A drip of blood slid from one corner of his smile. "There's no end to it, really—and therefore also no beginning. At least, not any that I can put into words."

When Illiaz looked up to meet Lux's gaze again, the blue of his eyes was, as always, that painful, too-alive shade of flame. "I don't know who you are, Lux," he said. He reached up to wipe away the drip of blood with the back of his hand, looking down at the red smeared over his skin. He laughed slightly, then immediately covered his mouth with his hand as more blood gargled forth. "...And I can't decide that for you. All I know about you is what you are to me, Lux—and that's neither your identity nor your history."

Lux felt something in his stomach clenching. "So what am I to you?" He wondered if he'd asked that question before. Illiaz must have gotten used to having to repeat things with him by now. Maybe Illiaz even had all these conversations and interactions memorized, had them rehearsed and perfected.

"What are you to me?" Illiaz repeated, a cadaver dressed in blood and silk dark enough to hide the frailty of his form. "You're all that's kept me from killing myself for years." For whatever reason that made him laugh, handkerchief held to his mouth to prevent the blood from getting onto the carpet. The dark red was starting to drip now not just from his mouth, but also from his nose and eyes. They were painfully dilated and wide. "The only reason I'm still alive. The only reason I *want* to be alive."

A dryness filled Lux's mouth. "If that's the case…" He crossed over and crouched down in front of Illiaz, reaching out to touch the blood leaking from flame-blue eyes. "What would you let me do to you?"

He felt like he was dreaming. Since his dreams felt utterly real, he wondered if that meant this was actually real. He wondered how he was supposed to tell.

There were giant spidery legs tearing out of his own back, like he'd dreamt had torn through Illiaz; they waved in the air behind him.

Illiaz had tensed when Lux had crouched close to him, but now he relaxed, smiling with blood in his mouth and in his nose and in his eyes. "Anything you want to."

Lux wondered what would happen if he tugged Illiaz with him out into the light of the sun.

HIS NAME WAS Luxanthus Nkidu Madubabakar. He'd been the Second Prince of the desert kingdom of Ordyuk, called a Blessed warrior, and now he was a gladiator in the kingdom of Mythus's Arena, in which fighters and accursed monsters fought each other to the death. He was very, very good at killing the Accursed.

Only, there had been too many of them. And Illiaz was right:

protecting him greatly impinged on what Luxanthus was capable of. Luxanthus didn't care.

When Luxanthus's arm was torn off in order to keep Illiaz from getting hit, he still didn't care. He simply dismembered the Accursed and used its spiderwebs to reattach his arm the way the Accursed reattached their own limbs and healed their own wounds. He could feel the curse squirming in his flesh as it reattached his arm, turning him into an Accursed himself. He still didn't care.

With the accursed appendages that emerged from his body, his range was much extended, and it was much easier to defend Illiaz. And it no longer mattered if he got injured, since he could heal himself by tearing into the defeated Accursed with his teeth, taking in energy from their flesh and devouring their curses until his entire body was crawling with them.

The Accursed tasted disgusting—which must have been the reason why they ate humans instead of each other—but he choked them down anyway.

There were so many curses in his body and in his head. Something about it was addicting. He kept acquiring more and more, till he was doing it not just to heal himself, but out of an all-consuming hunger.

He just wanted to be powerful. Powerful enough to protect what he cared about. That was all he'd ever wanted. That was why he'd trained and trained and trained, at the cost of everything else.

But power always came with drawbacks. The loss of one's humanity first and foremost.

The smell of Illiaz's blood was tantalizing, and Lux leaned closer, saliva collecting in his mouth. He pressed a black-nailed hand bruisingly over Illiaz's shoulder, making him flinch. "I can do anything to you?" he asked, and moved close to breathe into his ear. "Even if it ruins this carpet?" Lux didn't recognize himself; but then again, he never did. He didn't have any idea who he was, and he didn't have any idea if he was awake or dreaming. He wondered which one would be more worrying.

Illiaz laughed beneath him, the blood on his breath wafting savory, salty, and sweet. "...I can't believe you."

Lux sat back, looking down at him. Something was crawling scorpion-like up his throat. Illiaz tensed when Lux got up and moved several steps away, hovering by the windows. He traced his fingers over the fabric of the curtains, the same way he'd traced them over the blood on Illiaz's skin. "What if I leave you?"

Illiaz pushed himself up to his elbows, and then to a sitting position, brushing a hand back through his hair and laughing wetly. "I'd prefer if you killed me before you left," he said, smiling with blood running like tears from his eyes. He let out another chuckle, arms around his waist as he spasmed with agony. "Otherwise, I'd have to do it myself." He grinned, dark red dripping down his chin. "And it would be so much less painful if you were to do it for me...." Another laugh, and Illiaz cursed when his blood splattered on the carpet, but then he only laughed harder. More blood and more dark tears.

Lux looked at him, feeling a settling in his stomach and a bitterness in his mouth. "It would be easy to break you." It would be far too easy. There wasn't any point in doing so, when Illiaz seemed to be disintegrating just fine by himself. Why should Lux help death when it was inevitable?

"I know." Illiaz smiled at the ground, blood-red tears running down his cheeks. His heartbeat was unsteady, his breath wet and gasping. "After all," he said, "I'll die even without you." When he looked up and met Lux's gaze, his expression was all spider mums and spider lilies. "Whether you find this fact ironic or not, I would have broken long before this without you...."

Lux just looked at him, abyssal. His stomach was cramping, and he wasn't sure whether he wanted to vomit or sink his teeth into Illiaz's skin. "What do you want me to do to you?" He regarded the pain that was threaded through every fiber of Illiaz's body and wished he knew what that felt like. His tongue darted over his lips, but his stomach twisted. "What do you want from me?"

Illiaz wiped at the blood leaking from his eyes. "I just want..."

He looked away, gaze first on the floor and then on the insides of his eyelids when he closed them. The smile that broke upon his bloody lips was not unkind, but nor was it gentle. "I just wanted to exist in your company, because with you I've never had to be Blessed." His voice was blood and self-deprecation. "And I...want you to remember me." He opened his eyes again, meeting Lux's gaze, his pupils dilated dark and wide, the thin band of iris around them a stunningly painful blue.

Lux wanted to swallow that color, and that color only.

"I want to be whatever it is to you that will allow you to remember me," Illiaz told him, smiling like the bloody remnants of a nightmare turned into a dream. "I want to let you do to me whatever will allow you to remember me."

Lux felt a sinking in his chest.

But of course Illiaz would ask the one thing of him that he could not give him. "You know I can't promise memory."

It was hard to tell whether Illiaz was laughing or crying as he shook, gasping out a weak, *"I know."*

Dim centipedes of sunlight crept on the walls. "Is there something you're not telling me, Illiaz?" His mouth was watering; he swallowed his saliva down.

Illiaz laughed at him, wiping blood from his smiling lips. "I thought you knew that there's a lot I'm not telling you."

Lux exhaled through his nose, carefully controlling himself. He amended: "Is there anything you're not telling me that I should know?"

Illiaz laid himself back down on the ground, curling on his side. "...No," he decided. "There's nothing you need to know."

"Not even to stay out of the sunlight?" Luxanthus asked.

"Ah." Illiaz's smile was dark with blood. "You finally remembered."

HIS NAME WAS Luxanthus Nkidu Madubabakar. He'd been the Second Prince of the desert kingdom of Ordyuk, called a Blessed warrior, and now he was a gladiator in the kingdom of Mythus's Arena, in which fighters and accursed monsters fought each other to the death. He was very, very good at killing the Accursed, and he'd been housed in the barracks with others like him.

Not everything they had him doing was gladiator work. They also had him cooperate with various experiments.

They didn't do anything to him, of course; he was too valuable as a Monster Killer. They only had him use his gladiator skills on others.

There was a youth named Chass. He had straight black hair and hazel eyes that slowly turned to gray as the experiments progressed.

Luxanthus was brought into the experiments because he was an expert at killing. They had him kill Chass over and over, in different ways each time, after which the boy would come back to life. There was a woman scientist who went by Haydie, and she'd ramble enthusiastically and take notes, muttering things about snake venom and certain concentrations.

It was not work that Luxanthus enjoyed. But he did it. He didn't have a choice.

If it wasn't him, it would've been someone else. He figured, then, that it might as well be him, because at least he could make sure that Chass would die with minimal pain.

Luxanthus had killed countless monsters. He had not killed humans before killing Chass.

The disturbing part was that it was the same.

"I'm sorry," he said to Chass. But he was good at what he did.

Chass smiled at him wanly and said, "It's okay. It hurts less, when you do it."

So Luxanthus nodded and killed him again.

In the end, he was just a weapon.

LUX NARROWED HIS EYES at Illiaz. "Keeping me ignorant. Is ignorance supposed to be bliss?"

Illiaz looked at him with dark red eyes through his pale hair. "...It's a simple fact that what you don't know can't hurt you."

Holding his bloody gaze, Lux smiled wryly. "What you don't know can still kill you, though."

Illiaz laughed at him. "Nothing I know of could kill you, Lux." He coughed up more blood, cursing as it splattered on the carpet, then laughing at himself and coughing up more blood, which caused him to laugh even harder, until he ended up vomiting, the contents of his stomach all red. There was nothing there but stomach acid and blood, and Lux could smell that it was all Illiaz's own: he hadn't swallowed anything but his own bodily fluids in who knew how long.

Lux watched him, tilting his head, feeling disconcerted since he couldn't tell whether or not this was a dream. It seemed like Illiaz had already coughed and vomited up more blood than should've been in his body.

"I don't think anything you know could hurt me, either, Illiaz."

Illiaz clenched a hand atop the dirtied carpet. "...Probably not," he acknowledged. His eyes were dark and wide, his grin full of both laughter and agony. "But I'm selfish, Lux; I'm so terribly selfish." He was grinning, grinning, grinning; just looking at him made Lux feel tired.

"It's not for your own sake that I don't want you to know, Lux— it's for my own. So please..." He laughed again, agonized and hollow and despairing. "Allow me this..."

Lux's mouth was dry, his stomach emptier than Illiaz's. "Allow you what?"

Illiaz laughed, coughing up more blood, and laughed harder until, in his agony, he began to cry. His tears were dark and bloody and he smelled, overwhelmingly, like a dying thing. "By the *deities* and all their *cruelty*, Lux," he gasped out, "my entire existence *hurts*." Whether he was crying through his laughter or laughing through his tears, it was impossible to tell. "Please," he gasped out, an anguished sound, *"make it stop..."*

"Is this why you wanted me here?" Lux knelt and held Illiaz in his arms, wondering at how alive he seemed even when so obviously close to death. Illiaz bleeding out looked far more alive than Lux felt with all his blood in his body, and Lux brushed his tongue over his sharp teeth and exhaled around the void in his chest. "So that I could kill you."

Illiaz's agony curled his body against Lux's, his weak fingers clenching uselessly around Lux's waist. He gave a hollow, bloody laugh, hacking up a lung with his words. "It wasn't the only reason..."

"But it was one of them." Lux felt something in his chest settling like sand let free on the wind.

Illiaz was snickering, his body pressed close enough that Lux could feel the degrading of Illiaz's organs through his clothes and flesh. He was falling apart like a flower bouquet in the water. "...So what if it was?"

Lux exhaled, brushing a hand through Illiaz's hair, watching the white tendrils spill through his dark fingers and catch on the rough edges of his black nails. "You could've told me. I would've known my purpose, then." Perhaps then Lux wouldn't have been so lost and hollow. Maybe then he would've cared.

"If I'd told you," Illiaz mumbled the words against his chest, in between shudders and blood-wet coughs, "would you have remembered?"

Lux's fingers stilled their ministrations for a brief moment before starting up again. "Probably not."

"See?" Illiaz laughed, the sound hollow of mirth but full to the brim with pain. "I just wanted..." He shook his head against Lux's chest, exhaled shakily. "My life has never been my own, Lux. So I at least want my death to be."

Slowly and unsteadily, Illiaz raised a pale hand, fingertips darkened and glistening with crimson blood that he traced viscously over the skin of Lux's cheek. When he looked up to meet Lux's gaze, it was with blood-crying eyes and a blood-leaking smile. "Would it be okay if I asked you to kill me?"

Illiaz was all pale flowers crawling with dark millipedes, now. The scent of blood filled the air, and Lux felt only an empty and jaded hunger as he pulled back slightly, lifting a hand to brush his fingers over the bloodied skin of Illiaz's neck, the erratic and weakened pulse of Illiaz's heart beneath his fingertips.

"Is here fine?"

There was blood sticking Illiaz's eyelashes together like starpoints as his eyes lowered, face dark with blood and a smile on his lips like a lunar eclipse. "Thank you."

When Lux's hand hovered over Illiaz's skin it looked dark; when it pressed over Illiaz's blood it looked light.

Leaning in, Lux dug in his teeth and tore out Illiaz's windpipe, swallowing Illiaz's last shuddering gasp.

Lux wiped his mouth with a gold-clad arm, looked down at Illiaz's empty eyes, leaned back down and sank his teeth back in, tossing his head to the side as he stripped the meager flesh from Illiaz's bones.

Even covered in blood and gold and with a stomach full of tendon and skin, Lux felt light and empty. When he was done, he wiped his mouth of blood and looked toward the curtains with their edgings of sunlight.

Illiaz had told him to stay out of the sun.

Now, though, he didn't exactly have a choice.

But even as he reached for the curtains, there was something in him that made him want to turn around and head straight back into the dark.

HE NO LONGER REMEMBERED his name. He no longer remembered that he'd been the Second Prince of the desert kingdom of Ordyuk, called a Blessed warrior, and now he was a gladiator in the kingdom of Mythus's Arena, in which fighters and accursed monsters fought each other to the death. He didn't even remember that he was very, very good at killing the Accursed.

All he knew was that he needed to protect Illiaz. Illiaz, who had been the one person in all his life who had looked at him and seen a person who had feelings, as human rather than as divine or monstrous.

Now he really was a monster. But that was okay.

Even when he was locked away somewhere dark, it was toward Illiaz that he kept crawling.

Part II: Illiaz

Illiaz Fonhellansicht's life had never been his own.

His earliest memories were of watching his mother skillfully manipulate makeup to conceal the dark marks of her bones bruising through her flesh, the dark smudges beneath her eyes from nights made sleepless by pain. She added the missing life to her face by coloring her pallid cheeks with blush, her pale lips with rosy lipstick. She used dark eyeliner, mascara, and eyeshadow of iridescent violets and blues to draw all the attention to her eyes—which, in her entire appearance, were the only parts of her that looked truly alive.

He had memories of watching in the mirror as she did the same to him, feeling her hands butterfly-soft on his face, icy cold against his burning skin. The tickle of her soft lilac hair as she leaned in, the delicate ministrations of her long pale fingers as she carded them through the deep iris-purple of his hair, the scent of her perfume: a heady blend of rose and sandalwood, sprayed on too thickly in an attempt to smother the smell of the blood on her breath.

They arose each morning looking deathly, but by the time she was done, they were so enchanting it took his breath away. They were glowing and full of life, glitter brushed on their skin and eye-lashes, shimmering with their every movement, their every blink.

His father was the head of the largest trade company in the Mythusian Empire, and they had access to the greatest selections of goods the entire world had to offer. With their makeup and their vibrant silks—light and soft so as not to burden their weak bodies or chafe their sensitive skin—they were colorful and embellished enough to rival peacocks and golden pheasants.

His mother would hug his burning body with her icy cold arms, the happiness and love in her smile bright, the light in her eyes warm and compassionate.

His life had never been his own.

"I'm going to leave you soon, my dear Zaz. This body won't last. Yours won't, either."

His every breath and movement were painful, and he could tell they were even more painful for her, when she allowed him to see the truth. It was something she only ever allowed him to see.

"I'm not going to hide from you that which is your own exist-ence and reality, Zaz."

She showed him how to move with fluidity and grace, how to carry himself in a way that looked painless and relaxed, how to turn an agonized grimace into a dazzling smile, and how to laugh in a way that was musical and wouldn't draw blood.

"Why was I born, Mother?"

Unlike all the boys he met at the parties they threw and attend-ed, he was not being raised to take over the family's business at his father's passing.

He wouldn't live that long.

"Because your father and I love each other. And we love you, Zaz. You know that, right? We love you so much."

And oh, how well he knew. It used to make him happy. The way his mother would light up when she saw him. The way his father would kneel down to his height and bestow him with exotic gifts from far-off lands. The way people's eyes would be drawn to him whenever he passed by or entered a room.

Their adoration filled him with pleasure, such that it didn't matter that breathing hurt, that he was too weak to play with the other boys, that he could hardly eat anything before his stomach churned and writhed like it would twist its way out of his abdomen. None of it had mattered.

"If you look more closely, Zaz, you'll find that this curse of ours is a blessing in disguise."

He needed only say someone's name, and he could get them to do whatever he wanted; none could resist the power of his charisma. He and his mother may have been weak in body, but their words held divine power.

That divine power came at a terrible price.

When Illiaz was young, there were times when he would be utterly exhausted, when all he wanted was to sleep and yet he couldn't because everything hurt. He would feel that he was truly suffering then, and he would cry while his mother would hold him and hush him, while his father would be there with soothing salves and calming teas, hands that were not so icy cold.

His parents never once apologized to him for his condition. He was grateful that they didn't; it would have undermined all sense of purpose in his existence. He was the same as all the wondrous birds and flowers in the Fonhellansicht greenhouse: he was there to make others feel happy and elevated when they looked at him. His existence was like art and music—wordless pain turned into ineffable beauty.

Being that for other people used to make him happy.

He admired his mother greatly, the way she'd lived kindly and beautifully through the agony and degradation of her body. He'd watched as she'd become progressively thinner, as her lilac hair became lighter and lighter till it faded to white, as she changed her lipstick from rosy pink to a dark red to conceal the blood that started staining on her lips. He'd watched as she'd grown weaker and weaker until she could no longer leave her bed, watched as she brushed away their concern with graceful, trembling hands, watched as she laughed up blood and smiled through reddening eyes.

She was beautiful even in death, skeletonized, with her colorless hair spread all around her, head tipped to the side, the trickle of blood from her mouth slowing, her eyes closed, frosty eyelashes against bone-pale, violet-bruised skin.

He'd known that she was going to die—just like she had known that she was going to die, like they'd all known, and like they all knew that he would be dying, too—and so he hadn't cried for her. Not with the way she'd smiled at him just before she passed, like she was content to be living the life she was.

He didn't cry for her, but when she went perfectly still and didn't open her eyes when he placed his small hot hand over her frigid cold one, he'd cried as he realized what death truly meant: that death meant gone and never coming back.

He cried because he realized that once he died, he'd never get to do any of the things he enjoyed doing anymore. He'd never again feel the sun on his skin. He'd never again look up at the night sky with all its stars. He'd never again see the awed stares directed his way or hear the stunned gasps he caused others.

Worse, he'd never get to experience anything that he hadn't yet.

He'd always wanted to see all the places that the exotic gifts his father brought him came from, but he'd always been told he couldn't go because it was too dangerous. He'd always held out hope that one day he would be stronger, and he would be able to go—but his mother had only ever grown weaker, and had died. Just like he was going to. And once he was dead, he would never get to see any of those places.

The fear of death had resounded in him with a bone-shaking, breath-stealing, head-snapping impact.

He'd been nine years old at the time. He'd changed, after that.

He became filled with a profound sense of emptiness. He felt keenly the way he was burning away, without having any power to slow the ravenous flame. To live was to burn, and to die was for that burning to be extinguished. He could feel that flame of living eating its way along the short wick of his lifespan.

Why was he alive?

What was he living for?

Was it worth it?

What would his life have been worth when it reached its end?

In his mind was a lapping ocean of questions, and he wandered within the boundaries of his world looking for the answers.

He searched for them in his reflection in the mirror, as he brushed his mother's makeup over his skin, concealing the dark marks of his bones bruising through pallid flesh, the dark smudges beneath his eyes from nights made sleepless by pain. He added the missing life to his face by coloring his wan cheeks with blush, his pale lips with rosy lipstick. He used dark eyeliner, mascara, and eyeshadow of iridescent violets and blues to draw all the attention to his eyes—which, in his entire appearance, were the only parts of him that looked truly alive.

He saw his mother there, in the reflection of his face and the movements and effects of his ministrations. But he was not her, and carrying on as her echo was no reason to live.

He searched in the gardens and greenhouse, wandering with his fingers trailing over flowers with petals as soft and colorful as his silks and satins, trailing his eyes over the peacocks and the golden pheasants on which he'd always based the meaning of his existence. But was it enough to be a beautiful ornament? Was it meaning enough for existing just to cause people to smile when they looked at him? For them to feel like their hearts had taken flight and were soaring away with their breath?

Who ever knew that the world could be so beautiful.

He was so incredibly empty, like a burning flame.

The sensation of hunger was the only thing that filled him. It settled in his stomach and tingled his tongue, relaxed the tension of what little muscle was wrapped around his bones beneath his skin and the softness of what fat he retained only by virtue of his youth.

He wandered through halls and rooms he'd wandered countless times before, trailing his fingers over statues and treasures whose beauty had once filled him with delight, and wondered why they now only filled him with pain. Like this body of his. Where had the magic gone?

(It had all drained out with his mother's life and the illusion of endless possibility.)

Life was limited. Possibility was limited. His existence was finite.

The realization of that was painfully hollow. It was an emptiness that he wanted to fill up with something.

He searched within the confines of his world but couldn't find anything. Maybe if he looked somewhere else, he thought. There was nothing here but empty reflections of his vacant self in the surfaces of gold and silver plates, in faceted gems, in calm water ponds with lotus and koi, in dewdrops on flower petals, in the iridescence of gold and blue feathers.

He wondered about the worlds all those beautiful things had come from. Maybe some of the other treasures those places held would be answers to his questions.

His father had returned from a long caravan trip a few weeks after Illiaz's mother's death. He'd frozen when he'd heard the news. Then he'd turned and walked out of the house.

Illiaz had watched from the window as his father had wandered in the garden, picking flowers here and there, gathering them in a tanned hand till he had a large, brightly colorful bouquet. Then he'd walked to where Ari's grave was, set the bouquet down atop it, and stood there while the sun'd slowly traversed the sky.

Then he'd come back inside, his eyes red but dry.

They'd all known she was going to die. Every time Philamon had left on a trade venture, he and Ari had kissed goodbye like it was the last time. And finally, it had been.

Illiaz's father presented him both with the gift he'd gotten especially for him as well as the gift he'd originally intended for Ari. Then they ate dinner together, while Philamon narrated adventures and stories of his travels, and Illiaz ate his food slowly and carefully to conceal how it made him feel sick. He asked questions, uttered exclamations, and laughed in all the right places.

His father finished with a pregnant pause, watching him with steady brown eyes beneath graying eyebrows.

"Are you okay, Illiaz?"

They both knew he was asking about how Illiaz was dealing with Ari's death.

Illiaz had smiled at him.

"I'm well, Father."

They'd all known she was going to die. They'd all been prepared for it, and the preparations of the Fonhellansicht family had never failed them.

Three days later, Philamon was already preparing to leave for his next trade venture. The Fonhellansichts had always been a practical, business-minded family.

Maybe the problem was that Illiaz wasn't any different.

He saw the possibility of answers in the exotic presents his father had gifted him: in the small carved jade dragon, ornamental stone with a poetic suggestion of movement and sense of sleeping power; in the decorated box that Philamon had intended for Ari, with a crank that caused the box to produce music as if from a tiny metal piano and to slowly spin the dancing figure atop it. Illiaz saw the possibility of answers there, and he approached his father with cool certainty growing in his too-hot chest.

"Father, I want to go with you on the trade caravan."

"That's not possible."

"Why not?"

"It's too dangerous. I've told you that before."

"Dangerous? Which means I could die?"

"Indeed."

"But, Father, I'm going to die anyway."

"The risk that you would die en route is too high. Losing you that way would not be worth it."

Illiaz's life had never been his own.

"But if it would be worth it to me?"

"Would it be?"

"I've heard such wondrous things about Ordyuk. I want to see it before I die."

"You won't see it if you die en route."

His father always was incredibly practical.

"But I might not die en route. So there's a chance I'll get to see the city. But if I don't go, then it is absolutely certain that I won't see it."

"I can't lose you, Illiaz."

Illiaz had always known that he did not exist for his own sake—he had always existed for that of others.

"But I would be with you, wouldn't I? Think about it, Father. If you take me with you when you travel, even if I die somewhere along the way, you'll get to see much more of me than if you leave me here. I might die here while you're gone. Just like Mother did."

"I can't lose you too, Illiaz. I can't."

"You're going to. No matter what, you're going to. So wouldn't you rather spend what time I have with me? When I die, I don't want to be alone here in this house. Without having hardly seen anything of the world. Without having hardly spent time with you."

"Do you understand what you're asking of me, Illiaz?"

"For my life to, despite its inevitable shortness, be one that was worth living. Don't tell me I can't go just because I'm ill, Father—you could die during your travels, too. If it's dangerous even for people who aren't ill, then it's not any different for me just because I'm fated to die young."

His father had been the one to teach him to read, had given him books and scrolls and encouraged his literacy and learning. And Illiaz had read—he'd read about philosophy and about the world. He felt he'd found an answer there, about how he could live a life that was fulfilling rather than empty.

"Illiaz, life is about weighing risk with reward. As you are, the risk you'd die en route to Ordyuk, or in the city itself, is far greater than any reward either of us could reap from your accompanying me."

"But, Father—"

"However, your illness does not fate you to live a life constrained by it. There are ways to increase your strength and stamina. I can hire you an instructor. If, after enough time, it's confirmed that you're strong enough, you can accompany me on my travels."

His father had always been highly practical.

"Thank you, Father. I will do my best to improve myself."

It gave him a goal and therefore a purpose: he wanted to become strong enough to be allowed to travel. Toward that end, under the instruction of a martial arts master his father hired, he trained carefully to improve his strength and endurance, and to calm his mind and focus his breathing and thoughts; to control his perception of the pain in his body and the way he responded to it, both mentally and physically.

His father had clearly put great thought and research into the choice of martial art and instructor. The martial art was one whose primary goal was avoiding and disabling your attacker with minimal physical effort, and the instructor—an old man by the name of Aodhealbhach Sinngan—was endlessly inspiring to Illiaz with the power his martial art gave him despite the frailty of his age, his coffee-stained-paper skin and creaking bones.

"Tell me, Sinngan, what is it like to grow old? Since I'll never experience it myself."

"Only if you tell me what it's like to be young, my dear Illiaz. It's been such a very long time since I was young, you see."

Illiaz looked at his instructor, at the inset crinkles around his mouth from thousands of smiles; the watery light of his eyes like deep, dark pools; the jagged scar over his left brow and cheek; the white hair and beard like hanging moss grown over his face. Illiaz turned his gaze up to the sky and tried to feel that which was inside him and pumping through his veins.

"It's scary," he uttered finally, feeling that truth's fingers, cold as his mother's, curl around his throat. "I've seen so little of the world, and I understand even less."

The sky was blue with clouds that day, streaks of white shifting in incomprehensible patterns. In their travels across the sky, the clouds merged into each other, stretched thin, broke apart, and then arced into each other again, forming different pictures every several seconds.

"That sounds far more like age than youth, my dear Illiaz. Youth is bold and fearless, because youth is blind; with age you open your eyes. And what you see when you do makes you afraid."

The sky between the clouds was such a fathomless blue that it felt wont to swallow him should he stare too long into it.

"How do you keep going when you're afraid?"

"Because the only other option is to stop, and that's even more terrifying."

"What makes it worth it?"

"That's a question each man can only answer for himself, Illiaz."

"What makes it worth it for you?"

Sinngan's laugh was like the beat of a chant: meditative and quieting with a reach that went bone deep.

"Why, getting to meet people like you, young Illiaz. My time with you has enriched my life. I am grateful for all this time we have spent in each other's company, learning from each other."

"Do you think I'm ready? Am I strong enough now to travel and see the world?"

Sinngan's fingers, like gnarled wood, stroked his dry, mossy beard.

"Nobody is ever truly ready for what the world will bring. But you are certainly stronger than you were. And you're as strong as you're going to get staying here. The only way for you to get stronger is to go out into that world that nobody is truly strong enough to survive."

That made Illiaz smile.

"Because we're all going to die in the end, right? Nobody ever survives everything."

"We all have a death. Some of us try to outrun it, only to be taken down from behind at the last. But I can feel the way you cradle yours close to you, my young Illiaz."

"My life is not my own. But my death will be. I want it—"

He felt his smile to be as incomprehensible a movement to him as the shifting of the clouds in the sky; and he laughed slightly, the way his mother had taught: like bells, and without drawing blood.

"—I want to feel fulfilled, when it embraces me. Does that make sense?"

"Your soul may very well be older than mine, my dear young Illiaz."

"I somehow doubt that, honestly."

Sinngan laughed at him gently. It was a soft feeling, and Illiaz smiled in return.

Something in Illiaz's chest felt lightened after his talks with his instructor. The training itself had given his mind something to latch on to: given him a reason to want to get up in the mornings despite the exhaustion; a reason to try to fall asleep at night despite the pain; a reason to force himself to eat despite the nausea. He still questioned the world, but it had felt somehow more okay. Less like he might slip and fall off the face of it or cut his abdomen wide open on a sharp edge.

When he wasn't carefully training his weak body, he read voraciously—as if the stories, thoughts, and sights which were kept alive in the words on those pages could fill the emptiness inside him.

When he wasn't training or reading, he took to cleaning and reorganizing the items in the mansion. He wiped the dust and cobwebs from the statues, polished the tarnishing silver or the gold jewelry, and then used the polished jewelry to decorate the dusted statues. It soothed the ache of his soul to imagine all the distant places they came from, and to think that one day he'd be able to see them for himself. He felt, too, as he reorganized his surroundings, that if he had to stay in this place, then he could at least change the way things looked within it. Things that had been as they were in that house for years didn't have to stay that way; and this thought reassured him, even while pain thrummed through his body like a plucking of harp strings.

His body always hurt; that was never going to change, except with death.

He was thirteen years old when he was allowed to join his father on the trade caravan. His once dark, iris-purple hair had become a mid-toned, bluish lavender. When he shook people's hands, the heat of his skin made them pause, but no longer made them flinch.

With every passing day, his skin grew imperceptibly colder, and his hair grew imperceptibly lighter. The change was unnoticeable, like the blooming of a flower, like the movement of the sun through the sky, like the passage of scenery as the caravan traveled: the swaying grasses, the looming trees, the shimmering waters, the golden sands. The rumbling of the carts was like thunder in his bones and made them bruise more darkly through his flesh, such that he needed to use thicker layers of makeup to conceal their existence. But the cities they visited had no shortage of new cosmetics with which to add the missing life to his face, no shortage of new garments with which to cover and adorn the painful existence of his body's fragile corporeality.

(Maybe, if he was dazzling enough, he'd be able to make time itself pause.)

The young tightrope-walker he'd seen balancing between two buildings in the middle of a rainstorm in Ordyuk had filled him with wonder, as had so many other things. Buildings and people and customs, animals and plants and goods, all the likes of which he'd never seen before, would never have been able to imagine, and had no words for. Sights and experiences he could not begin to describe. They cut him open from the inside.

There was a sensation within him like sand falling through a small opening from his lungs into his stomach. Time lapped at him like the river rapids against the sides of the boats. Sometimes, when he looked down, the ground swayed like a pendulum beneath his feet. He only knew he wasn't dreaming it because his mind was not so great as to be able to imagine all this in the world before him. It had to exist outside him, because things so wondrous could never have existed in his head.

He kept walking, staying steady. He felt heavier than stone, but he made sure to move as if he were as light as air. Crowds parted before him and people bowed down at his feet at a word, at a gesture. He smiled like he had the sun behind his teeth and moved with a grace that beguiled even snakes. Days were filled with pain, sunlight, and song; nights were filled with agony, darkness, and the crackling dance of fire. Sometimes the darkness was made up of clouds, thick and pressing almost close enough to touch, offset only by the warmth that sense of closeness created; sometimes the darkness was made up of the fathomless distance between him and the stars, offset only by their colorful winkings and by the way they were gathered together, as if there were some cosmic order to their chaos.

It was on such a night, when the distance above him felt like an eternity, when he had the conversation with his father. The questions had been burning on his tongue like sparks, and when he went looking for his father, he found Philamon tending the camp's fire. The flames' ravenous crackling threatened to drown out his voice.

"Father?"

"Yes, Illiaz?"

He'd sneezed red earlier that day, and he'd had to rinse out his mouth with rosewater. Afraid the blood would still be detectable on his breath, he'd sprayed on his rose-and-sandalwood perfume even more thickly than usual. Its scent still filled his nose even now, hours later and above the fire's acrid smoke. The aroma reminded him vividly of his mother, of her death and the blood trickling from her mouth to stain white sheets.

He looked at his father, knowing that Philamon must be able to smell the perfume. He hoped that he couldn't yet smell the blood.

"Is it worth it? Is it worth it to raise me when you know I'm going to die young, in the same manner as Mother? Raising a child who won't be able to carry on the family business after your passing? Raising me knowing that you're going to lose me?"

He'd been wondering for such a long time.

His father exhaled; and when he inhaled to speak, Illiaz couldn't help but fear that he could smell the blood beneath the roses and sandalwood.

His father spoke softly.

"I asked your mother the same thing, when she said she wanted to have you. I was 14 years older than her and already 32 when we married. I'd long cast aside the idea of producing an heir. I'd never actually planned to marry, in all honesty. But your mother...I loved her. And I could deny her nothing."

Philamon looked into the fire, its flickering light dancing on his sun-tanned, wind-rugged features, on his graying blond hair and the dry light of his eyes. Illiaz had never seen his father look like he might cry, not ever.

"It was no secret that she was going to die young. I wanted only to ensure that the rest of her life was as pleasant as it could be. I didn't want to have a child, as I was afraid she would not survive it— but she wanted to have you so badly. And I could deny her nothing."

Philamon's lips were curved in a smile that Illiaz didn't then understand. Only years later would Illiaz recognize the enigmatic expression that so often graced his father's features as one of soul-deep, heart-scarring love.

"We knew that if we did successfully have a child, that child would likely share her fate. But your mother said to me: 'What is the value and worth in a life? Is it its length? Is a life not worth living simply because it will be short and full of pain?'"

Philamon shook his head, and Illiaz laughed like the clear tinkle of so many small bells. "That's all any human life is in the end, isn't it? Short-lived and full of pain."

His father looked at him with the firelight flickering over the deep brown of his eyes.

"Your mother always said she was grateful for all her pain, because it made it so she could never forget that she was alive. She felt it so keenly—everyone around her couldn't help but feel it keenly, too: that sublimity of life. You're just like her, in that way. Raising you as my son has given me a joy beyond anything I'd imagined possible."

Illiaz's father gazed at him softly.

"Illiaz, we all live for ourselves, but we find our worth in other people. In that which is not directly tangible: in memories, in dreams, in legacies. In the ways we've left our touches on the minds and hearts of others. That, in the end, is the only thing that preserves us and gives us worth."

Illiaz looked at him, and then away, into the fire and its leaping, devouring flames: flames that reduced wood and bone to smoke that drifted away and dispersed into nothingness. Illiaz felt that same nothingness in his chest, in the rise and fall of his lungs and the beating of his heart.

"Do you ever feel empty, Father?"

There was no silence with the fire cackling as it devoured, but there were moments without words.

"I used to. Before I met your mother. Once she entered my life, nothing felt empty anymore. Even now that she's gone, my life isn't empty. Because I have you."

Illiaz smiled beatifically, without the faintest idea why.

"But Mother is gone. What will you do when I'm gone, too? Won't you be empty again then?"

"No."

The answer had come quickly, and Illiaz had looked over at him curiously.

"Since your mother's death, I've realized...I still have my memories of her. I still see her in the marks she's left. In me, and in others. It will be the same with you. You and your mother have made this world a more beautiful place just by existing in it, Illiaz. I hope you realize that: even when you're no longer in this world, it will never be a world in which you did not exist. It will forever be a world that's been touched by you. I don't think I'll ever be able to feel empty in a world where people like you and her have existed."

His father had met his gaze with an unfathomable certainty. Illiaz didn't understand it, but it had made him feel secure, like the wrappings of a blanket, and he leaned against his father's shoulder, Philamon putting his arm around him and hugging him gently close.

"You're warm," Illiaz realized.

For all his life, everyone else had always felt cold.

It seemed he'd finally become colder than they.

His father's arm tightened slightly, then loosened again, and his thumb brushed gentle circles over the ridges of bone comprising Illiaz's shoulder. Illiaz sighed and closed his eyes.

He fell asleep there, against his father's side, and woke up in the morning on the mattress he'd been allotted in one of the covered wagons, his father's mattress empty but still body-warmed beside his. When he'd stepped outside and made his way back to the fire, his father was engaged with a map and a compass, talking to his second-in-command, and the other men of the caravan were gathered around and making the place lively, their laughter dancing jigs in the air. They grinned when they saw him, beckoned him over and cheered.

"Another night without calamity! Thank Murkudu, Deity of Good Fortune! Praise Lasamu, Deity of Protection! Praise the Blessed One who brings us the deities' favor!"

They bestowed upon Illiaz a plate of fruits and lightly cooked meats. He smiled, ate what little he could, and threw the rest into the fire as an offering to the deities.

Philamon may have let Illiaz accompany them because he did not have it in him to deny Illiaz his desire to see the world before his death, but for the men of Philamon's caravan, Illiaz was their token of fortune and protection, Blessed by the deities and a guarantee of their safe passage.

Never once, since Illiaz had joined the caravan, had they been attacked by bandits or suffered significant hardship. He was, they lauded, the first sign of the deities' favor since the Great Calamity had ended more than three decades before.

And so Illiaz smiled like he had the sun behind his eyes, concealed the bruising from his outward-clamoring skeleton with cosmetics and silks, and smothered the scent of the blood on his breath with perfume.

He couldn't hide it from his father, though, who knew. They'd both known, from the beginning, that Illiaz's partaking in the caravan's travels would not last long.

"Illiaz, I will allow you to accompany me. But only for so long as your body is strong enough. You must understand, I cannot stand by and watch your condition be needlessly exacerbated...."

Sixteen nearing on seventeen years old, with his hair a shade of gentle lilac and his skin gaining a coldness that made people drop his hand as soon as they took it, he knew that his days of traveling were approaching their end. He wondered when his lilac hair would, like his mother's, become a perfect lily-white.

Everyone died; his approaching death didn't make him special.

It was so hard to remember that when everyone always looked at him like it might be for the last time.

He wondered why, after all these years of looking his death in the face, the two of them weren't better friends. It wasn't because he was afraid of his death. That dark nonexistence didn't scare him; it would be just like sleep. A sleep from which he would never again awake to pain.

Why it was so difficult for him to look his death in the eyes was due to his fear that, when it embraced him, he wouldn't have lived a life worth having lived. And if his life wasn't one worth living, why wait for his death to come to him? Why not kill himself and get it over with? Everything hurt him. For what reason did he suffer it?

He laughed when he made the realization that he was holding out under the hope that he might find something that would make everything worth it. That he might find something, somewhere, that would make him truly glad to be alive. It felt wrong to give up when there might be a possibility that he'd find that something.

But he hadn't found it in the travels he'd been allowed. And he most certainly wouldn't find it in that house once he'd been forced to return to it.

And return to it he did.

The only option left to him was to search within the boundaries of the city on whose outskirts the Fonhellansicht mansion lay, and he chuckled darkly to himself at how discouraging that was. Still, he had nowhere else he could look, and for whatever incomprehensible reason, he couldn't bring himself to give up his hope.

He went out as often as his pain-racked body allowed. His death hovered over him, above and slightly behind, tracing its cold fingers over his neck, wrapping loosely there like a collar he'd never escape no matter where he went.

The city of Mythus, capital of the Mythusian Empire, wasn't really any different from all the other cities he'd visited. Not in essence. There were shops with things he neither needed nor desired, markets with food he couldn't stomach, people whose bodies hurt him when they accidentally knocked into him. The only difference was the Arena with its gladiator fights.

For years he hadn't been allowed to attend them. Now, they couldn't keep him away.

There, where death and the struggle against it were turned into a glamorous spectacle, was the only place where Illiaz felt truly at home. His death, which held him from behind with arms close and cold, found company in the death of others and laid its head against his shoulder, humming.

He felt kinship while watching the gladiators fight to the death. They were staring their demises straight in the face, unable to look away. The only difference, he thought, was that they, unlike he, were able to fight against their end's embrace.

Another step, another stab of pain; another step, another stab of pain; another step, another stab of pain; blood in their mouth and on their breath—they were just like him, those gladiators fighting to their deaths.

He realized he was probably the only one to envy the gladiators so severely. But he did envy them. He envied them their strength, their skill, their capacity to fight against their death, and the fact that, when they died, they did so quickly, with meaning and with celebratory fanfare. The gladiators died to the sound of applause and cheers, rather than to sobs and tears. Illiaz envied them that dearly. He thought it would be beautiful to have people cheering at his death. Such a life, where people celebrated its end, would surely have been a life worth living.

Maybe it was due to the irregularity of his attendance that it was so long before Illiaz saw the gladiator Luxanthus Nkidu and finally found what he'd been looking for: a reason to delight in being alive in this world.

Luxanthus Nkidu was purportedly the star of the gladiators, and, watching him, it was easy to see why. The youth was covered in gold ornaments, wearing nothing else but loose black trousers tight only at the waist and ankles. His skin was of deep bronze, his hair shone like tiger's eye, his defined musculature was like that of statues carved to be the absolute epitome of human beauty, and his skill was, even to the inexpert eye, absolutely unparalleled. He made battle look effortless. There was such a fluid and uninhibited grace to the way he moved; watching him, one forgot entirely that what he was doing took any kind of effort at all.

Luxanthus Nkidu may have been a prisoner in that Arena of death, but he was freedom alive and breathing.

They never pitted him against other gladiators. It would surely have been a boring battle, if they had, for he surpassed all other humans. When he made appearances in the Arena, it was only to fight the dreaded Accursed.

The Accursed were terrifying. The whites and irises of their eyes were red, their teeth sharp, their bodies capable of sprouting large, weaponized arachnoid appendages. They moved like starvation-insane animals, without any thought or feeling except to feed. They were human, and yet not; they were beasts, and yet not; they were forces of nature, and yet absolutely unnatural. They were monsters.

And yet the gladiator Luxanthus Nkidu, who couldn't have been older than Illiaz's eighteen years, made them look weak; he killed them so easily, so effortlessly.

'Monster-killer' everyone called him. It was the name cheered in the stadium, whispered with reverence on the streets. After his victories, the crowds, roaring and cheering, showered him with jewelry and ornaments, and he adorned himself with every single piece. The only items he didn't put on were the earrings, which he pocketed; there was already a pair of gold rods hung from holes in the lobes of his ears, and he didn't appear to have piercings for more.

Illiaz was keenly aware how much effort it took to make one's movements look light and effortless when one was weighed down. How much weight must all the gold and jewels Luxanthus Nkidu wore amount to? Illiaz could barely walk under the weight of light silks.

But by the deities, Illiaz tried so hard to make it look like moving was nothing. As if he were a bird, and even his bones were hollow. As if his movements were danced by the air instead of weighed down by it. He tried so hard to look as light as Luxanthus Nkidu did, covered in gold and blood, flipping through the air, skidding his sandals in graceful lines through the dirt, and leaving footprints when he leapt high above the ground as if it had tossed him. The cut of Luxanthus's sword was a crescent glint of silver, slicing the Accursed like the moon cutting the night. Monsters lunged at him like inevitable demise, and he evaded them like a deity, effortless in his immortality. His every movement was like music made corporeal: a harmonized symphony, rises and falls that lifted the soul beyond the reach of the earth.

A light awoke inside of Illiaz for the first time he could remember. Watching Luxanthus Nkidu, Illiaz felt that all the pain of life was worth it, just to be able to exist in a world that held someone like the monster-killer.

Illiaz could feel his body degrading. The taste of blood never quite left his mouth. But the press of his bones trying to break free of his flesh now made him feel like he could almost fly; the ache of his joints now made him feel as if he could jump to the moon.

He lived for the next time he could watch Luxanthus Nkidu fight. It hurt him so deeply he choked on it; blood in his mouth, and he smiled with it. Like Luxanthus ended each fight with blood all over his skin and none of it his own.

Illiaz was going mad in his head. He was dying in his body. He wasn't even sure if he was real—he felt so intensely like he was capable of anything and yet nothing at all.

After one gladiator fight, as the rest of the audience was leaving, he swung his legs over the wall and then jumped down into the Arena (it hurt like a curse—but *everything* hurt). He walked toward the closed doors through which the living gladiators had walked, through which the living monsters had been herded, through which the dead gladiators and monsters had been carried.

The guards barred his path.

"Halt! What do you think you're doing?!"

Illiaz smiled. "My name is Illiaz Fonhellansicht. I would like to be Luxanthus Nkidu's patron and houser. Please, allow me to pay all expenses regarding him and to house him at my manor when he is not needed in the Arena."

Perhaps life was nothing more than a dream of the dead, because that's what he felt like, standing there and smiling: dead and dreaming.

If the guards' spears had pierced him through, he'd have been saved an awful lot of pain and suffering. But they didn't; he didn't know if it was his offer of money, or his family's name, or the look in his eyes—he didn't know what it was, and he didn't care, as they led him to people who led him to people who led him to people who acquiesced to his request. They could hardly have refused him, not with the power he had over them as soon as he spoke their names.

They brought out Luxanthus Nkidu dressed in chains. The dark iron clashed horribly with the gladiator's gold. It made Illiaz feel sick.

"Take those off."

Luxanthus's eyes, too, were gold.

The guards fidgeted.

"But—"

"Take them off."

They took the chains off, and then held them out.

"Here. You should at least hold on to them."

Illiaz kept his hands by his sides. The metal was thick and heavy; Illiaz was too weak to carry it. They didn't need to know that.

Without saying anything, he turned and walked away.

Luxanthus was behind him; the gladiator smelled of frankincense, myrrh, cinnamon, cardamom, saffron, sweat, and blood.

"If I may ask?"

Luxanthus's voice was deeper and sandier than Illiaz had expected.

"What is it?"

"Where are we going?"

"Where do you think?"

Luxanthus didn't answer, and Illiaz couldn't bring any more words onto his tongue; they died in his throat and at the edges of his mind.

They were, both of them, silent. With every step, Illiaz felt like he was dying. And wasn't he? Slowly but surely.

When he stumbled, Luxanthus didn't hesitate to catch him. All Illiaz had the strength to do was laugh, and he barely had the strength enough for that.

"Thank you."

Luxanthus was silent, but the smell of him was everywhere.

Illiaz was cold. He remembered his mother carding fingers like bone through his dark violet hair, brushing blue and magenta around his eyes. He remembered her smile and the light illuming her pale cherry-blossom hair and eyelashes. He remembered her frigid touch on his face.

"All that is beautiful is ephemeral, my dear Illiaz."

He remembered the way he'd had to fight back shivers.

"Then what isn't? Ephemeral, I mean."

He remembered the blue of her eyes turning away, her decorated eyelashes drifting sparkles like dust to her cheeks. He remembered the soft, resigned parting of her rose-painted lips.

"Only that which is terrible lingers despite the passage of time."

Back then, Illiaz hadn't understood.

Now, with Luxanthus's apathy burning behind him, he realized what it meant. It made his lips curl bitterly.

How badly he wanted to be *terrible*. But he was far too weak and far too deathly; all he could be was graceful, delicate like a flower. He was no burning sun like Luxanthus.

And so he walked, pale and cold, and tried to make it look as if he were floating, beautiful and unearthly like the moon.

Days and nights in his mind, like feathers tumbling in the breeze. He was terrified to fall asleep, and the darkness he avoided pooled purple and black beneath his eyes. He concealed it with foundation, the same way he concealed the bruising of his bones.

Luxanthus walked the halls with tear-wrenching jangles of gold, sunlight catching on his jeweled metal adornments and strong, muscular lines.

"Luxanthus."

"Yes?"

"Do you mind if I call you Lux?"

It had to be a nickname, else Illiaz's Blessing would come into effect. And Illiaz selfishly wanted the gladiator to be there by his own consent rather than forced to remain by the power that was killing Illiaz from within.

"That's fine."

Illiaz laughed, and let his smile linger even after.

"Thank you."

"For what?"

The sun-gold of Lux's eyes pierced him like snake fangs. The shiver down his spine caused him pain—just like his breathing and his every step and gesture.

"For indulging me."

"It's not like I have a choice."

Illiaz smiled, feeling pale and thin like a crescent of the moon, not even full in his cold emptiness. He could've been knocked from the sky to the ground with the wave of a hand.

"Do you not?"

The gladiator could have no idea the degree of choice that Illiaz could have taken away from him, if he so chose.

"...I guess I do."

Lux was looking at him consideringly, and Illiaz could only smile back wanly.

He was dying, tasting blood and losing time. It scared him. It terrified him. It horrified him. It destroyed him. Yet in those moments when Lux could have left him and yet did not, choosing of his own accord to stay and humor Illiaz's conversation, Illiaz felt pleased. There were things that he could say to the gladiator that he could say to no one else, because Lux was the same as he: both blessed and cursed by the deities.

Everything about Lux was gold, and Illiaz could taste the metal in the blood on his teeth. The sunlight was shining warm on them, but Luxanthus's eyes were brighter, richer, deeper.

"What am I to you, Illiaz?"

There were flowers all around them, budding, blooming, and wilting, their aromas thick in the air. Illiaz smiled—not despite the fact that he was dying, but because of it.

"A selfish indulgence."

Lux's brow was creased as he regarded him.

"You don't hate me."

Illiaz tilted his head, lilac eyelashes streaking sparkles through his vision.

"Why ever would I hate you?"

"Everyone else does."

The gladiator looked troubled. Illiaz tilted his head, lilac hair falling over his right eye like a gossamer veil.

"Why do they hate you?"

Lux's sun-gold eyes on him, brightly illuming, were far too searching.

"For having what they don't. For being what they aren't.... I make people jealous."

Light purple hair was drifting into Illiaz's eyes, tickling his face like the sunlight on his skin. "I'm not jealous. I could never carry what you do. And truthfully, I don't want to."

He may have been envious once, yes; but that was before he'd realized that Lux had no more control over his gifts than Illiaz had over his own curse, and that a life as a gladiator couldn't be a particularly happy one at all. Lux may have had advantages that Illiaz did not, but he also had misfortunes that Illiaz did not. Every advantage, Illiaz had realized, came with its own disadvantage. Like the way that Illiaz's gift of influencing people to do what he wanted if he used their name came with incessant pain and an early death. Lux's skills in battle, therefore, no doubt also came with their own pains, which couldn't be any better than Illiaz's own.

Realizing that, Illiaz was no longer jealous; he just enjoyed Lux's company, because he wanted to spend his time with someone who didn't pity him. Only an accustomed killer like Lux could be so irreverent in the face of death.

Sun-gold eyes on him, and he wanted to bask in that unsentimental gaze forever.

What a shame that Illiaz had to die.

His hair was such a pale lilac, so close to white. All in his face and in his eyes, reminding him of his mother and her lifeless form. He smiled with his death, like a flute-charmed snake behind his teeth.

Those sun-gold eyes on him narrowed. "You're not jealous?"

Illiaz wanted to laugh. He didn't. He kept the snake trapped carefully behind his teeth and smiled. "No."

"Why?"

Those sun-gold eyes on him, keen and searching, and Illiaz smiled with closed lips so that whatever those eyes found wouldn't be the blood staining the cracks between his incisors and canines. "You make fighting look so easy, and that looks terribly hard. I wouldn't want to have to do that."

Lips carefully, gracefully kept closed, he shrugged like it didn't hurt him. He wanted to speak, but the moment felt too delicate; like a dry, dead flower that would crumble to dust at a touch.

He was, he thought, happy, then and there. In that moment. In all the moments Lux offered him.

But happiness, like everything that was beautiful, was ephemeral.

Illiaz thought his time with Lux would end with his death. He'd never thought that he'd have to *live* with the pain of losing him.

People were calling the event the Second Calamity.

A horde of the Accursed, hundreds upon hundreds of them, led by Jajul, the Deity of Chaos itself, in a human form. They attacked the city, killing and devouring indiscriminately. The streets had run with blood and the air had echoed with screams. It had only lasted a day and most of a night, but by the time it was over, more than half of the populace had been slaughtered. All the other survivors were calling it a calamity, a tragedy. They cried, gritted their teeth, sobbed, clenched their fists, yelled, shook, ranted, or else stared at the world with void expressions and dead, blank eyes.

But Illiaz was painfully aware that everybody died. And the dead, in Illiaz's view, deserved no sympathy, no pity. It was only the living who experienced pain. And the victims of the Second Calamity had died quickly, with only having suffered seconds to perhaps a few hours of the terror of death before all that suffering was alleviated. They had not spent years watching their death grow within them, waiting for it to finally become larger than they.

Illiaz had been watching and waiting all these years. But still he was alive, and all these other people had encountered their own death as a complete surprise.

He should've died during the Second Calamity. When the Accursed had attacked the Fonhellansicht manor, if Lux hadn't protected him, Illiaz would certainly have died.

But Lux had been there, and so instead of dying, he'd watched Lux become an Accursed and yet keep fighting, gathering more and more curses into himself as he devoured the other monsters. By the end of the Second Calamity, Lux, with bloody eyes and arachnoid appendages writhing from all over his body, had been nearly unrecognizable. He'd even begun devouring humans. And yet he hadn't eaten Illiaz, despite Illiaz's weakness.

The anti-Accursed warriors had finally stopped Lux's rampage, stabbing him through the brain and then carting his body away.

Illiaz had thought he was dead.

Curled up in his bed without the will to move, Illiaz could feel his own skeleton within his body. It felt like it was trying to break out, as if it couldn't wait for the rest of him to rot and for it to be all of him that was left.

Now that Lux was gone, there were only people who pitied him left. Why should he continue acting for them? He might as well let his body degrade. What was the point of trying to take care of himself?

When his father had said that the world was a more wondrous place even after someone had existed in it, he had evidently been lying; now that Lux was gone, the world had never been more painful and distressing.

"I'll see you in the afterlife, Lux."

Illiaz was no stranger to pain. He'd felt pain before, had been in pain his entire life—but nothing like *this*, and he didn't understand it. The world felt empty and bleak, as if when Lux had gone, he'd taken all the light with him. But that should have been okay. Because Illiaz was used to that, too. He'd lived his entire life before Lux without him. So why should anything be any different, now? Maybe he felt like a bird in a cage, emaciated, its wings clipped so that all it could do was cling to its perch, clean its colorful feathers, and sing. But that was how he'd always felt. Even when Lux had been there. Why should it now be this intolerable?

Illiaz looked at his reflection in the mirror, stripped of its makeup so that his bones showed through, his skull beneath his skin framed by cherry-blossom hair. Dark bruises around his eyesockets with blue eyes looking out of them, framed by pale eyelashes. He watched his bloodless lips move.

"This is the worst day of my life."

The laughter bubbled up dark and hot in his chest, up his throat, clots of it in his mouth. It was never going to be getting any better. He tried to think of the future, and all he saw were rows upon rows of days as dark and empty as this one.

Lux was never coming back.

From that point on, every day he lived was going to be the worst day of his life. No one else was like Lux. Lux had looked at him like he was art, even when he'd been coughing up blood. Even when, with fingers wet from his own sweat, Lux had reached out and cupped Illiaz's face, brushing his thumb over Illiaz's cheek and beneath his eye, wiping away the makeup to expose the deathly skin and dark bruising of bones beneath. Lux hadn't seen pain or death as ghastly. He'd seen them as something else. He'd been perfectly calm, perfectly relaxed, perfectly accepting. The same as he'd always been preceding, during, and after his every gladiator battle.

He'd looked at Illiaz in the exact same way.

"I don't understand how I haven't broken you, Illiaz."

Illiaz had tilted lilac hair into his face and smiled. "It's because you haven't tried to."

Lux had looked at him so curiously it had made Illiaz laugh, flecks of his blood on Lux's chest, and the gladiator hadn't moved to wipe it away. Illiaz had wanted to, except that just because there was blood on the monster-killer didn't mean that it was his. It didn't compromise either of their perfect images if it stayed there. And so he'd just smiled and let Lux wipe the blood from his lip, along with the lipstick that gave his bloodless flesh the illusion of life.

He didn't mind if Lux reduced his appearance to that of the walking death which he was; Lux was the only one who understood that death was not a terrible thing. Who was comfortable with that fact.

But now Lux was gone, and Illiaz didn't know how he'd survive the rest of the days of his life.

Instead of covering his lips with lipstick, one day, he simply picked at the dry skin until it bled. Blood was the color of life; goal still accomplished. He simpered at himself in the mirror.

He was so grotesque, and everything hurt. His entire body. His every movement. Even his breathing and the beating of his heart. It was difficult not to cry from the agony. Why, again, was he trying to hold the tears back?

Right, it would ruin the makeup around his eyes. Well, then why wear the makeup, if it was so easily ruined? He could just stop wearing it. Then he could cry.

Only, the crying didn't help. The crying hurt him, too. So what was the point?

He stopped crying. He stared at the wall. He tried to remember what he was supposed to do. What was worth doing. He tried to remember why he was alive. Why he existed. Why he was suffering like this.

He couldn't think of anything. It struck him like a revelation.

He was too weak to be a killer, though, even of himself. He tried, once, but it didn't work and his father caught him, and then all the sharp objects and mirrors were removed from the mansion.

He stared at the wall and waited for either sleep or death to take him. He wondered if he'd be able to tell the difference.

A metal plate was there on the bedside table, with the food no doubt caringly prepared for him, but it wasn't worth eating. He was hungry, sure—his stomach felt like it was devouring itself, and it probably was—but that held no significance. It hurt, but everything else did, too. Eating would also hurt.

He wanted to die.

Yet even his own death was outside of his control.

There were no mirrors, anymore, but his hair in his face was bone white. Just like his mother's had become. Death couldn't be that far off. The thought made him smile.

He remembered thinking, watching his mother's cadaverous body twitch and spasm with blood frothing from her mouth and her eyes opened sightlessly wide, that it would be kinder to kill her.

"Would you like me to end it quickly, Mother?"

She'd shaken her head and smiled through the blood, so he'd guessed that she was enjoying the pain. So he hadn't killed her, and he'd thought that, when the same fate was his, he'd understand.

Now that fate was indeed his, but he didn't understand at all. Why had she wanted to keep living with that suffering? He wanted his to end. It was such pointless, meaningless suffering.

His death was so close, now. He could feel its cold embrace around him, teasing bony fingers over his sternum so that he coughed up more blood into his opened jaw and cupped hands.

He never imagined that Lux was alive.

Even if he'd imagined that Lux was alive, he never would've thought he'd see Lux the way he did next: chained hand and foot, half-starved, blindfolded and muzzled with metal, hair oily and dingy.

The gladiator was shoved straight onto the floor and stayed

there, breath rasping through the muzzle and chest heaving. He lay on his front until the guard rolled him over with a foot. Then Lux had just lain there on his back, unmoving except for the heave of his chest.

Illiaz staggered to his feet from the bed with strength he hadn't known he still had in him. He dropped to his knees beside the gladiator, hardly daring to breathe. There would be dark bruises on his knees later. He didn't care.

"Is this really...?"

Lux hadn't had many scars before—only a few small, light ones—but they were all gone, now. His skin was utterly flawless. The nails of both his hands and feet were black.

Illiaz swallowed dried blood and saliva.

"I thought he was...?"

"Dead?"

One of the guards snorted.

"He would've been luckier, if that were the case. No—he became an Accursed so atrocious that not even lopping off his head can kill him. Still feels pain, though."

Reaching out with weak, trembling hands, Illiaz carefully pulled off Lux's blindfold. He inhaled sharply at the sight. Let out the breath painfully.

Lux's eyes were half-lidded, the whites bloodshot. With his gold irises and shrunken pupils, his eyes looked like butterfly wings. They stared sightlessly. It was disturbing, but also somehow stunning, and Illiaz could not fight back shivers. But maybe that was from the cold, kneeling there on the stone floor with the covers of his bed abandoned for the first time in—how long had it been? How long had he been like this?

How long had Lux been like this?

When Illiaz removed the muzzle, Lux gasped reflexively wider for air, his teeth all pointed and sharp, capable of tearing out chunks of a person with a bite. They were stained with old blood, and the smell of rotted meat was thick on his breath.

It reminded Illiaz of his mother, and he smiled.

"Why did you bring him to me?"

Illiaz's tears burned first his eyes and then his cheeks, lips, and tongue; their heat surprised him, because he was so cold. Perhaps he was crying the last of the heat from his body. His smile became salty with both tears and blood.

"Is it because I'm dying soon? You should know that everyone dies. There's nothing special about it."

He laughed, choked on the blood that came up from his lungs, and coughed, a hand coming up to cover his mouth. He grinned uncomprehendingly like a skull behind his skeletal fingers.

The room was dim, lit only by a couple of candles in their elaborate brass candleholders like small twining rose plants. It was a large room. But it felt small, now, crowded with the guards bearing the armor and regalia of the King's specialized anti-Accursed unit who had poured into the chamber.

In a sounder state of mind, Illiaz would have been distraught at them seeing him like this—emaciated, weak, and without any of his cover-up, the dark bruising of his bones visible starkly beneath his skin—but at that point he no longer cared.

He wiped the blood from his mouth with a hand, looking down and watching the candlelight flicker over the glistening red. He remembered watching the candlelight dance over the blood of his mother on her deathbed, just like this.

"I don't understand why you've brought him to me."

The guard scoffed. Maybe it was the same man, maybe it was a different one; Illiaz wasn't looking at them. His gaze was on Lux.

"You think this was done for your sake? Don't kid yourself, sick boy. He's been locked up in the dungeons, but he's so cursed strong that he keeps breaking out. Restraining him appears to be useless. He's a danger to society. It was decided that he should be brought here on the off chance that you can control him."

"You want me to control him? How do you mean?"

He wasn't sure if his Blessing would work on Lux when he was like this.

Those darkened, bloodied eyes stared half-lidded, dazed and sightless, like butterfly wings gracing the gladiator's face.

"He appears to have some kind of attachment to you, since he has been trying to return to this place and has said your name on more than one occasion. And then, of course, there's the power of your Blessing."

Illiaz swallowed thickly, closed his own eyes, and feathered his frigid hand lightly against the side of Lux's burning face.

He wondered, if he pressed his fingers in, whether he'd be able to feel the sharp teeth through the flesh stretching between the accursed gladiator's upper and lower jaw.

"—You think you can contain him, Fonhellansicht? You just need to keep him here and prevent him from losing it and going on a murderous rampage."

Illiaz's chest shook with something between laughter and sobs. He couldn't be sure which it was. They both hurt and tasted of blood.

"I'll certainly do my best."

It was absurd, wasn't it? That they were asking a sickly, half-animated corpse to contain a monster so strong that fortified cells and chains of the strongest metal couldn't restrain him.

"For the record, he's dangerous beyond belief now. So you better keep those chains on him."

The guard meant, of course, the thick chained cuffs around Lux's wrists and ankles. They looked heavy enough that Illiaz didn't think he'd be able to maneuver their weight enough to remove them, even if he wanted to.

"—Admittedly, they won't do much, should he decide to break them, but they're better than nothing. Your job is to make sure he *doesn't* decide to break them."

Illiaz gave an incredulous snicker, which turned into a wet cough that he reflexively covered with a hand.

"So my job is to make him *want* to be wearing them?"

His smile was dripping red behind his fingers.

"If you want to think of it that way."

The wry nonchalance of that answer made Illiaz laugh and dissolve into bloody coughs again. It said a lot about how informed the guards had been that they weren't alarmed. Whichever one was speaking continued on, as if Illiaz wasn't hacking up lurid bodily fluid right in front of him.

Illiaz appreciated it.

"Another note, Fonhellansicht: he's going to need regular feeding. You know that Accursed only eat human flesh, right?"

Illiaz smiled slightly, slowly lowering his hand. He looked down at the dark blood coating his palm.

"So what you're saying is...?"

"We'll have the flesh supplied to you. Due to the state of the city and empire, there's been an increase in crime since the Second Calamity, and what with all the victims from that disaster, there aren't enough morgues for all the executed criminals. This'll be putting their bodies to use."

Illiaz wondered if the guards expected any of that to bother him. "Everybody dies."

"Not everybody is eaten, though."

"Are they not? We're all eaten away by decomposers, eventually."

Invertebrate creatures like those whose enlarged appendages emerged from the Accurseds' bodies.

One or more of the guards huffed. There was a quiet muttering that Illiaz almost didn't catch.

"I suppose that's one way to look at it."

There was a sigh, then words spoken louder, in a tone that was flat and somber.

"As long as you know what you're getting into, Fonhellansicht. There's a chance he might not recognize you and attack. His memories appear to be compromised."

Illiaz's eyes widened slightly, and he let out a laugh that

might've been hysterical if it hadn't devolved so quickly into a violent fit of coughing.

If Lux didn't remember him, then what, by the deities, did they think he could *do*? He was so weak he could hardly stand. His relationship with Lux, whatever it had been, had been all he'd had. What kind of a deity-blessed miracle were they expecting from him? Would his power even work if Lux no longer remembered or responded to his name? And did they not realize that he was on the verge of death, and the more he used his power the faster it would burn up his life?

The deities had cursed him with suffering, and the fact that he lived on despite it made everyone around him believe that he was Blessed.

Is there really any difference between a Blessing and a curse?

"—In case the Accursed goes wild, you'll have a team of the anti-Accursed brigade at your disposal. They should be able to at least partially contain him until you can get through to him again. Assuming that you're able to at all."

Ah, there was some doubt.

"You must realize that this will be at the risk of your life, Fonhellansicht."

"Do I look like someone who expects to live much longer?"

When he coughed, his movements were too slow to catch the blood with his hand, and some of it splattered on Lux, on his chest and face. It made the accursed gladiator stir slightly, tongue swiping the flecks of Illiaz's blood from his lips. The pupils of his unseeing eyes dilated wide, the irises and sclera becoming so bloodshot his eyes looked like firebug carapaces. It made Illiaz's breath catch wetly.

Still he smiled, brushing the dark, unwashed hair out of those striking eyes.

"You may tell the King, or whoever entrusted me with this task, that I will do my utmost to contain Luxanthus."

"Far more lives than just your own are counting on you."

The statement was grave, but Illiaz just smiled. "And I'll take responsibility for them."

It wasn't like he'd live to fail their expectations; if he failed, he'd be dead before anyone else.

Some of the guards shifted slightly, uneasy at the sight of him. He must have been as ghastly as one of the soul-consuming monsters known as the Deathless, with their skeletal figures, feathery white hair, and soulless eyes. All he was missing were the wings.

"You may leave us alone, for now. It'll be better if it's just me."

He was wearing his beautiful, reassuring smirk. The confident one with a gentle, teasing edge.

On his uncovered face, deathly wan with the bones of his skull and the sleeplessness beneath his eyes darkly evident, the smile no doubt produced a much more eerie and disturbing effect.

"Trust me."

The guards, when they left, probably did so because they didn't want to be stuck in that room with two monsters.

Illiaz turned his attention back to Lux, feeling his breath go unsteady. He reached out, hovered his crimson-glistening fingers above Lux's atrophied abdomen. A single drop of blood fell to the accursed gladiator's skin, and Lux's entire body shuddered. Illiaz retracted his hand, closed his eyes so he wouldn't cry. He imagined he had a rose between his teeth and smiled.

"All I wanted was to die." His grin felt dark and thorned. "Was that so terrible of me?"

Illiaz remembered, as a child, picking bouquets of roses and watching them decay, keeping them in his room until they died, and then keeping them still. He used to have an entire windowsill lined with bouquets of long-dead roses. Their dried petals had fallen and scattered over the room, tracked by his aimless feet.

"Is it my fault that I was born this way? Is it my fault that I can't change that?"

The blood was pooled darkly red in the palm of his pale, skeletal hand, the candlelight dancing over it. It tickled his eyes to stinging and he smiled; he always smiled, no matter how much he hurt. He didn't know what else to do.

There was all this blood in his hand and so he tipped it into Lux's mouth, watched him drink it, stir, and lick his tongue over chapped lips and sharp teeth.

They were both gruesome now.

In Illiaz's head were memories of withered rose petals held between his pallid toes, the sun's death on the blade-edge of the horizon, bloodying the sky.

He laughed, like the breeze that had sidled in through the open window and stolen the wilted petals from his weak toes.

"Why did you protect me, Lux?"

His mother had walked with him in the garden, once, when she'd been well enough. She'd picked a rose, carefully removed its thorns, and tucked it behind his ear.

"Live just as beautifully as this rose, Illiaz."

The rose had died within days and become a wretched, ghastly thing.

Illiaz was so tired. Colorless white hair in his face, strands of it caught in his mouth. His fingertips, with the blood drying there, sweeping over Lux's chest. He wanted to lay himself down against Lux's searingly warm body; he was so tired and so cold.

"You lost your memories, they said?"

He ghosted his skeletal fingers over the ridges of Lux's ribs.

How completely Lux's presence changed everything.

Illiaz wanted to chuckle, but he no longer had the strength. He made do with a smile, as he always did, the impulse to laugh meeting its fate as an agonizing throb in his chest that joined all the others.

Illiaz wondered, not for the first time, why his requests were being heeded—why, for his entire life, everyone had always heeded his requests even when he didn't use their names and compel them to. They could've knocked him down with a push, bruised him with a touch—and yet they not only did humor his requests, but they

eagerly jumped to acquiesce. He had never understood it. He probably never would.

He reached out to brush a lock of dark hair out of Lux's face,
the candlelight bringing out every gleaming nuance of its brown
shades, even lank and oily as it was. The gold necklaces and beaded
collars Lux still wore looked too heavy for him now. His sharp teeth
peeked out from between the parched, cracking lips between which
he rasped air; his firebug-carapace eyes stared into nothing.

Being a monster suited Lux, Illiaz thought.

The emaciated state didn't.

There was too much blood choked up in Illiaz's mouth, and so
he let it drip into Lux's. It was more than he himself could swallow.
Lux had no problem doing so, drinking it with delirious and
benumbed starvation, back arching off the ground. The world scin-
tillated as if with dark butterfly eye-spots ringed with glittering gold.

When the world leveled out again, he was lying next to Lux in
that place of darkness and flickering candlelight, blood puddling on
the floor beneath his cheek.

How close was death to breaking out of him and enveloping
him? Illiaz thought he could feel its cold breath ghosting on the back
of his neck, whispering in his ear. He wondered if it was the deities
set on torturing him who kept his death at bay, or if his death was in
on it, too, and staying deliberately a hairsbreadth away.

He watched the drumbeat-throb of darkness and candlelight
through the parchment-thin skin of his eyelids.

"This all seems highly unnecessary, doesn't it, Lux?"

A weak chuckle danced razor blades in his chest, because that's
all their lives were: unnecessary pain, unnecessary suffering.

"I'm not going to say that I'm sorry you have to go through this,
Lux. I'm not going to feel sorry for your existence, because I'm glad
that you do exist, even like this...."

It struck him that maybe other people had felt that way about
him.

At least, he hoped they'd felt glad enough that he existed that they hadn't felt sorry for him. The only choice anyone ever had was to accept life or to hate it. Illiaz was far too tired for hatred. What else could he do but accept?

His world was all dancings of pain, the taste of blood and the smell of rose-and-sandalwood perfume twining with the scents of sweat and metal on Lux's skin, the sound of Lux's heartbeat overpowering his own and the sensation of the shallow and gasping rise and fall of Lux's chest, the sound of those breaths hissing through sharp teeth. Illiaz wondered if he was cruel but hurt too much to care.

Time was indeterminate; it was dark, and the candle flames fluttered with the wavering beat of his heart.

Eventually, one of the members of the anti-Accursed unit came back in and inquired into his progress.

"He hasn't regained consciousness yet. He seems too weak."

The thought of what Lux must have gone through to have ended up weaker than *he* was rather impressive.

The guard left, and then presently returned with a severed arm for Lux and a small bowl of blood pudding for Illiaz.

There was more than just the fact that he so often hacked up blood that Illiaz's mouth always tasted of it: because he was always losing that blood, the dishes the doctors had suggested for keeping up his strength were blood-based. He ingested blood and then hacked it up in a bloody, vicious cycle.

Picking at the black pudding with the provided fork, knowing that he had to eat if he wanted to stay alive and be strong enough to use his Blessing on Lux should it be needed, Illiaz watched the curled-up, accursed gladiator devour the arm, bones snapping between his sharp teeth and blood splattering on his face to match his bloody eyes. Illiaz wondered why Lux had done that to himself— saved him and become a monster.

A guard hovered in his peripheral; Illiaz smiled for the man without really looking. "Could you get me a mirror? I won't try to kill myself with it, I promise."

He'd never wanted Lux to end up just like him: full of so much pain he was numb with it, beaten down and dead-hearted with it.

Was that care? Illiaz wondered. He'd swallowed rose petals, once, because Lux had told him that he should eat but he'd been tired of the taste of blood. Now Lux had become a human-eating monster because he hadn't been willing to let Illiaz die. But for what had he saved Illiaz at the cost of his humanity? All he'd done was prolong Illiaz's suffering while guaranteeing his own.

Or maybe they'd both just wanted to devour. Was that care?

When the handheld mirror was produced, Illiaz glanced at his reflection. He looked at the bones of his skull bruising purple-black and purple-blue through his frost-layer skin behind half-translucent white hair, and tucked the mirror away with trembling, bone-irregular fingers. As gracefully as he knew how, he brought another bite of the blood pudding to his lips. The smell of it overwhelmed him, mixing familiarly with the scent of roses and sandalwood. He bit in and swallowed anyway, grinned instead of grimaced, chuckled instead of choked.

Lux had finished devouring the arm and was licking the blood from his fingers. The guard kicked him, and he hissed, tried to push himself up, and fell crashing back to the ground when the guard kicked his cuffed arms out from under him. The guard sneered, eyes dark, clear hatred in his gaze.

"He's still weak, at the moment. It'll be best to keep him that way. You realize what's going to have to be done to him when he loses control, right? He heals fast and creepily as *curses*, now."

To demonstrate, the guard stomped the heel of his boot into the bone of Lux's nose, crushing it. Lux wrenched away with a strangled sound of pain. As Illiaz watched, small arachnoid appendages, their carapace surfaces shiny black with traces of gold iridescence in the candlelight, emerged from Lux's skin—like miniature versions of those he'd seen on the Accursed in the Arena and during the Calamity—and straightened his nose, stitching his flesh back together with spiderweb-like threads that faded into the skin as it healed, a rippling beneath the skin as presumably more of the accursed appendages did the same with his nasal bone.

The entire process was over within seconds, the arachnoid appendages disappearing back beneath Lux's skin, stitching it with spiderweb-threads behind them so that when they faded and the flesh healed, it was as if they'd never been there.

A painful shudder moved through Illiaz, bringing an overwrought grin to his face.

The guard was utterly callous.

"When the accursed bastard loses it, it's going to take extreme violence to subdue him again."

Oh, but the dying bird that was Illiaz's heart had wings. Illiaz brought a bite of the black pudding back up to his teeth and scraped it off the metal spoon, forced himself to swallow.

"I understand."

He'd do what he could to make sure that violence wouldn't be necessary—that Lux wouldn't have to suffer any unnecessary pain beyond that of existence itself—but he wasn't sure how much longer his own body would last. What would they do to Lux once he was dead and was no longer there to contain him?

"Do you really?"

Illiaz let out an incredulous laugh, turning his head to fix him with his bloody smile.

"Do you really doubt me?"

The guard stared at him, parted his mouth, and then closed it and averted his gaze.

Illiaz smirked, feeling complacent. "You may leave us."

The guard left, and then it was just he and Lux again at what felt like the end of the world. Except that it wasn't.

Illiaz forced himself to finish the blood pudding, forced himself up, forced himself to stagger to the bathroom, forced himself to draw his makeup over his face. He barely made it back without collapsing.

Lux was still wearing his gold jewelry. Illiaz carefully, strenuously removed it so Lux could better move, starved with hunger as he was. With significant effort he placed the gold ornaments into several woven baskets and then pushed them underneath the bed.

He returned to Lux's side and carded skeletal fingers through Lux's dark hair until the gladiator's bloodshot eyes finally focused on him. Then he smiled.

"Do you remember anything, Lux?"

Lux stared at him with eyes from which most of the blood had cleared, so that they once again resembled veined insect wings. Illiaz smiled.

"I'm Illiaz. Illiaz Fonhellansicht. Do you remember me?"

Lux stared at him with his gaze as uncomprehending as butter-fly eyespots. Illiaz smiled.

"A simple nod or shake of the head will suffice."

Lux stared at him and slowly, carefully shook his head, as if it took great effort. Illiaz smiled.

"No? That's okay."

It wasn't. It hurt him all the way through his flesh to his bones. But still, Illiaz smiled.

Maybe the pain was enough. Maybe there wasn't any feeling that wasn't pain.

All beauty was illusion; and Lux was still beautiful, even as a monster.

So Illiaz smiled.

OVER TIME, Illiaz would become familiar with the iridescent black-and-gold arachnoid appendages that emerged unconsciously from all over Lux's body and crawled over his skin. They wrapped around him like so many centipedes and millipedes, of all different sizes from tiny worms to giant pythons, emerging and then burrow-ing, sewing up the flesh they tore through with glittering strands like spiderwebs.

At times, the iridescent limbs of exoskeleton would twine

around Lux like the gold jewelry with which he used to adorn his body, and he'd look at Illiaz from within the crawling mass with eyes as emotionless as the patterns of insect carapaces.

Illiaz had seen the cursed appendages in the Arena and during the Calamity, but other Accursed had only ever exhibited a handful of them—never anywhere near so many as Lux, who at times seemed to be covered in hundreds, if not thousands. It made the gladiator look dead, like a corpse being devoured, and it gave Illiaz shivers because he related.

Maybe it was because there was, for the first time, someone in a worse state than he, but Illiaz found himself trying to make up for Lux's morbid state. He forced himself to eat, forced himself to sleep, forced himself to engage in light exercises. Because of that, he grew measurably stronger. The deterioration of his body slowed and even reversed slightly, and he felt well enough to move about the mansion and venture into the gardens. He covered his deathly appearance with makeup, and he chewed rose petals to smother the stench of blood on his breath, though it couldn't seem to do anything about the taste in his mouth.

He'd used to wear light clothes so as not to accentuate the deathly pallor of his skin. Now, he wore only dark clothing so as to hide the staining of blood.

None of the illusion of life that he drew back into his appearance dulled his keen awareness of his death. If anything, it made him even more afraid of it. Every time he succumbed to sleep, it was a small death that he happened to be fortunate enough to wake up from.

He had Lux stay in the same room as he, share the bed with him, lie next to him—partly to make sure he was there to calm Lux should he fall into a fit, but mostly because he was afraid of dying alone.

He slept next to Lux in the king-sized bed, but he did not ask for the gladiator to hold him. He was terribly self-conscious of the way his cold body was reaching the temperature of a corpse.

Sometimes, though, he would awaken with some of the accursed arachnoid appendages wrapped around him. He figured that was okay; their hard, smooth exoskeletons were as without warmth as he was.

The arachnoid appendages were, for the most part, benign. Most of the time when they appeared, it was to curl around Lux's own body, protectively or supportively. They became violent only when he was provoked or desperately hungry—the ironic thing being that the out-of-control appendages were the primary drain on his energy, with how they constantly tore through his flesh and healed him again.

They would also become violent whenever Lux was exposed to sunlight.

He'd always used to like standing in the sun, when he was human. Whether he would seek sunlight subconsciously from a desire for warmth, or whether he did it consciously because he was aware of the way the sunlight made him in all his gold jewelry glow, Illiaz had never known. But the gladiator had always used to seek out sunlight in which to stand.

Now, they kept all the curtains tightly closed, because the sunlight made Lux hiss like a cockroach and drop to his knees clutching his head, the arachnoid appendages erupting violently from his flesh to flail senselessly, striking at anything that came close.

That could happen, too, if the human flesh he was fed was too obviously from a human; Lux's psyche didn't seem to have fully accepted the new development of his body, and even without his memories, he seemed to recognize that there was something abnormal about eating humans. Recognizable human body parts caused a part of his mind to crawl out of its grave, wreaking some kind of internal mayhem. They'd tried feeding him other kinds of meat, but he'd spat them all out as if they were fetid. The only viable option was for the human bodies to be cut into unrecognizable slabs of meat, removing the skin and bones.

Whenever Lux went wild, flailing and destroying blindly, not even Illiaz using his name could get through to him. But perhaps, as close to death as Illiaz was, he no longer had the necessary life energy with which to make use of his Blessing. It was hard to tell, when he was filled with agony, whether or not he used it.

Lux would have torn apart the mansion if the anti-Accursed unit weren't there to step in. It appeared that damaging his brain was the only way to get the madness to stop; head injuries took by far the longest for the insect-appendages to heal, and seemed to require the most resources to do so. Nothing less could faze him, injuries to any other part of his body being healed almost immediately. But as soon as he was stabbed through the brain, the insect-like appendages retreated into his body in order to repair the damage, save for the few that wrapped around him like a protective, blade-proof cocoon.

The consequence of the brain damage was, of course, that Lux was continually forgetting everything. While the appendages could repair his brain to a functioning state, they didn't have the power to restore memories.

It was what pained Illiaz more than anything else: that Lux had not only forgotten him from before, but kept forgetting him; that once Illiaz was dead, Lux almost certainly wouldn't remember him.

He missed the way Lux used to look at him like he was art. The way Lux used to relax slightly whenever he saw him. The way his presence had made Lux smile. He missed the way Lux had grinned with warm laughter in his golden eyes when the gladiator had been delighted by something he'd said. He'd always known that Lux didn't feel much—that had been one of the things that had so attracted him about the gladiator, since he himself was always in so much agony, while Lux had always seemed so free of everything, even pain—so it had always thrilled him whenever he'd made Lux's eternal apathy crack.

Now, Lux only looked at him blankly, or else with forlorn curiosity, depressed suspicion, or resigned confusion. Illiaz hated it. The way Lux looked hopeless and lost, like he'd given up. Like he didn't care about or feel anything. Illiaz hated that he could no longer make Lux smile, that Lux neither remembered him nor felt anything for him. The only reason Lux didn't leave, it seemed, was because he didn't feel anything about it either way; he didn't care to stay, but neither did he care to go. Staying was the easier of the two.

Lux, after each time he lost control and had to be stabbed through the head, didn't remember Illiaz, and he didn't remember their conversations. And so they repeated—introductions, explanations, questions, answers.

Doing the same things again and again, having the same conversations again and again, always ever-so-slightly different enough to make his reality skew slightly to the left. Slightly different wording, a different location, different lighting, a different part of his body hurting, Lux's posture held a different way. The same conversations, just slightly different. Sometimes Illiaz felt like he was going mad.

Only occasionally did a version of a conversation they'd had dozens of times end up, unexplainably and inexplicably, drastically changed.

"Who are you to me?"

The question had thrown Illiaz off, the first time Lux had asked it, and he'd stared at the accursed gladiator for a long moment before he'd finally managed to smile and answer.

"An admirer."

Lux had been watching him upside down from where he was doing a handstand on the stairwell banister, apparently simply because he could. Illiaz had lightly told him to make sure he didn't fall and injure himself. Sometimes when the insect-like appendages emerged to heal him, Lux didn't seem bothered by them; other times, he regarded them with such shock and surprise that his mind made a break for it, landing him in another episode of uncontrolled violence.

It was safer if Lux didn't get wounded.

"So are you admiring me right now?"

Lux, with his wrists chained together, was doing a handstand on the banister with his hair all like bronze flames reaching for the ground and his butterfly-wing eyes beating. Illiaz wanted to laugh.

"Yes."

"Then I don't see what the problem is."

"Lux, I never told you not to do what you're doing, or to come down. In fact, quite the opposite—I told you to make sure you don't fall."

Butterfly-wingbeat blinks, the defined muscles in Lux's arms and abdomen shifting minutely beneath his skin as they worked to keep him in place.

"When you put it like that…"

The question was easier to answer the second time.

"Who are you to me?"

Lux could no longer stand in the sun, only exist in the dark, but in the dark Lux still sought out the light. He was like a moth drawn to flames.

He had sought out a puddle of candlelight, but at Illiaz's approach had turned to regard him in the darkness. The candlelight was on half of Lux's face, one side lit and the other dark. On the dark side, only his eyelashes caught the candlelight, making them glow gold around the darkness of his shadowed eye; on the lit side, his eyelashes were dark around his eye's illuminated veins of red, shadows of his eyelashes visible on his golden iris.

All Illiaz had to think about, the second time Lux asked the question, was whether to change his answer or stick to the same one he'd given before. It was hard to think with the way everything in his body was hurting.

"…An admirer."

Lux was stunning, even with his eyes full of blood.

It was even easier to answer the question the third time; Illiaz already had his answer and his decision to stick with it.

"Who are you to me?"

Lux was standing there with his muscular edges and planes

defined all in shades of shadow and moonlight, looking out over the balcony railing, shirtless with accursed appendages crawling over his skin like the legs of spiders and scorpions. They tore in and out of his flesh as he stared serenely out over the gardens, turning his head up to look at the distant and illuming darkness of the sky—the color of the bruises that Illiaz's bones pressed into his skin, smattered with coruscating stars like the glitter Illiaz brushed around his eyes.

Illiaz shivered. Looking up at the night sky gave him the same sensation as looking in the mirror and realizing he'd forgotten to put on his skin-colored foundation before applying all the rest—the blush and the eyeshadow and the glitter—and it repulsed him, while at the same time taking his breath away: because Lux looked striking standing beneath it.

Illiaz's voice almost cracked when he spoke. "An admirer."

Lux had glanced back at him, and Illiaz wondered what all those arachnoid appendages felt like, crawling iridescent black over Lux's skin, tearing apart his flesh with soft sounds and sewing it back together with silver, moonlight-catching threads.

The two of them could only go outside at night or when it rained. Lux seemed about as bothered by this as he was by the accursed appendages shredding and stitching his skin: all placid, unfeeling acceptance.

"An admirer? What is it you admire about me?"

Illiaz's throat was so dry he could hardly breathe.

"If I had to distill it down to one thing…it's your approach to life: the way you don't seem to perceive the endurance of pain as suffering."

Lux had blinked those utterly black eyes at him, shiny like the carapaces of scarab beetles, and looked back over the silver ground, the silver flowers, the silver trees, all of it edged in soft charcoal-dust shadow. "Pain as suffering, huh? I guess it's true that I've never thought of it like that."

Illiaz watched him, weak to the point of being almost unable to draw the moonlight-saturated air through his lungs.

"If I may inquire, Lux?"

The accursed gladiator turned those scarab-beetle eyes back on him.

"If pain isn't suffering to you, then what is it?"

Lux shrugged his black-crawling shoulders, turning his face up to the night sky. His eyes glimmered in the luminescent dark. "Pain is just the body's way of telling you that you did something wrong or have been doing something wrong, and that you need to change what you're doing in order to become better. It's information. It's useful."

Illiaz felt a softness inside him like something rotting. "I see."

By Lux's logic, Illiaz's entire existence was wrong.

No wonder they had entirely different understandings of the nature and meaning of pain.

It was harder, the fourth time, to answer that question from Lux:

"Who are you to me?"

The sun had gone down, and they'd ventured into the garden. The sky was threatening rain. Illiaz had tucked a blue lotus into Lux's hair, behind his ear, because it looked good there.

Illiaz was no longer sure what he was to Lux.

"...An admirer."

Lux's hand had risen up, touched his cheek where Illiaz's skeletal, warmthless fingers had brushed him in their retreat, moved to carefully brush his own fingers over the lotus's delicate, warmthless petals.

"Why the flower?"

"Why not?" Illiaz was so tired. "If it bothers you, you can take it out."

The fifth time was harder still, because by that point Illiaz no longer understood what he was saying, or why he was saying it.

"Who are you to me?"

Lux, licking blood that he'd stolen from Illiaz's lips.

"...An admirer."

By that point, he didn't have any idea what else he could possibly say.

By the sixth time, Illiaz no longer cared what he said in response—Lux was going to forget it all, anyway.

"Who are you to me?"

Lux looking down at him, large arachnoid appendages impaled in the walls and floor all around Illiaz, and Illiaz hadn't moved or tensed, had only relaxed and smiled. He'd sort of been hoping he'd die.

"An admirer."

None of it was going to matter, in the end.

After that Illiaz lost count.

"Who are you to me?"

"An admirer."

"Who are you to me?"

"An admirer."

"Who are you to me?"

"An admirer."

Illiaz had taken to cleaning things, reorganizing things, like he had when he was younger. Even though his mind was in pain-filled chaos, it seemed that it would be okay as long as the mansion—as long as his surroundings—were clean and in order.

Also, Lux had a way of attracting insects and spiders. He would be standing there watching them crawl over his fingers, his hands, and up his arms. Sometimes he'd be laughing with them crawling over his face, the skin around his eyes crinkled; sometimes he'd be shuddering with his eyes blown wide. Sometimes it made him go wild.

Illiaz paid special attention to clearing away the spiderwebs and any food or plant matter that could further attract bugs.

When Lux had been human, he'd slept moderately and lightly and had been dependably active, spending most of his waking hours training or meditating. Now, his sleep patterns were irregular: he either wouldn't sleep and would just lie there staring up at the ceiling, or he'd fall into a deep, dead-to-the-world sleep for unnaturally long hours. Often, too, his sleep would be disturbed by dreams that seemed to cause him great distress. He never screamed or yelled, but he would sometimes sit bolt upright with wide eyes or he'd bite and eat the flesh of his own hands and arms.

When he was conscious, there were times when he'd stare vacantly, his eyes open but as dead to the world as if he were asleep. But there were times, too, when he was lucid, almost the same as before he'd become Accursed. He would engage in physical training, and his conversation would be normal aside from his lack of memories.

Other times, he would follow Illiaz around like a dog, watching him with varying intensities of curiosity, from utter lack of care to desperate desire to understand something, but he would be almost nonreactive to Illiaz's attempts at conversation. Still other times, he would wander about the mansion by himself, looking around either idly or with the curiosity of a child, and his thoughts when Illiaz questioned him were especially peculiar.

"How did they die?"

Lux was looking at the suits of armor that lined the halls.

Illiaz shook his head. "They didn't."

Suits of armor had never been alive.

"Oh." Lux's fingers twitched at his side. "So that's why they still move."

Illiaz had no idea what Lux was talking about. He often didn't. He was never quite sure if the problem was Lux's broken mind or his own agony flaying his thoughts to shreds.

Sometimes when Lux was in such a curious mood, Illiaz would be the one following him around, watching with varying degrees of curiosity from fascinated to despondent; other times it was far too painful, and Illiaz would let him wander alone and would preoccupy himself with cleaning and reorganizing the mansion full of all the myriad gifts that Philamon had brought back from his trade expeditions.

Once there was a crash and a horrible *crunch*, and Illiaz, following the source of the sound, found Lux lying at the bottom of one of the grand flights of stairs with the arachnoid appendages fixing his broken neck, moving his unnaturally bent vertebrae back into place, and then stitching up his skin from the outside.

Illiaz stood over him, for once the one who had to look down. "...What happened?"

Lux blinked up at him, eyes calm as butterfly wings. "I fell down the stairs."

"...How?"

Lux was the most graceful and well-coordinated person Illiaz had ever seen, not to say anything of the incredible strength he had on top of that.

The accursed gladiator blinked at him, sclera veined through with red and irises of gold, his black pupils neither large nor small. "I was walking with my eyes closed."

"...Why?"

"Because I discovered that it scared me."

Illiaz just stared down at him, blinking in return. *"Come again?"*

"Walking with my eyes closed."

The accursed appendages finished repairing Lux's neck, and he shook his head slightly, as if to shake away a layer of dust. Still lying supine on the ground at the bottom of the stairs, he shrugged.

"It was fine as long as I could hold the picture of the hall in front of me in my mind and imagine where I was and where I was walking. But as soon as that image faded away and I no longer had any sense of my surroundings, it became frightening. That was a feeling. I'm not used to feeling much."

He looked up at Illiaz easily. Flat, butterfly-wing gaze.

"When you're numb and unfeeling most of the time, flashes of emotions are like thunderstorms. Out of the complete darkness and silence, feeling fear was like a brilliant, earth-shaking crack of lightning."

Lux was smiling, then. Illiaz felt like his every heartbeat was rending him apart from the inside: relentlessly, forcefully, mercilessly pumping the blood through his veins to keep him moving, keep him feeling, keep that blood spilling into his lungs and rising up into his throat, his mouth, places where it shouldn't have belonged and yet made itself at home.

Illiaz wondered if he'd ever felt anything like Lux was describing. A bright, awing crack of radiance. That wasn't like what Illiaz felt at all.

What Illiaz felt was like a constant barrage of painful, overwhelming hail.

"That sounds beautiful, Lux."

"It was."

Lux looked wistful. The expression was serene, and so Illiaz smiled, because it was so rare to see the accursed gladiator like that.

"Hence, I take it, why you kept walking with your eyes closed in order to feel that lightning-crackling of fear, and ended up falling down the stairs."

Lux beamed at him with a kind of happiness, as if he were delighted that Illiaz had understood him. "Precisely."

Every time Lux touched him, he left dark fingerprints on Illiaz's skin. And still it made Illiaz smile. "You're really something, Lux."

No one else had ever touched him like that; no one else had ever dared to.

Lux did, and not even because he dared. He simply didn't care. Illiaz didn't disturb him at all. Didn't awe him at all.

Apparently, that cracking of lightning was addicting, because Lux kept closing his eyes and not letting it stop him from walking forward.

He ended up crashing into and breaking some of the statues, knocking off stone heads and limbs. Eventually, there wouldn't be a single statue with its body intact in the entire mansion.

The poor statues.

The thought made Illiaz laugh, because he'd never had such a thought about anything living.

Maybe he only related to dead and lifeless things.

There was something wrong with him, Illiaz thought, and laughed harder because that was painfully obvious. He was, after all, incurably sick.

He remembered that there were doctors who'd tried to cure his mother. All their attempted remedies had never made her better. They'd never made Illiaz better, either—all they'd ever done was prolong his pain.

There was another question that Lux would almost inevitably ask each time he awoke with no memories, an uncharacteristic brittleness to his voice: "Why aren't you scared of being destroyed by me?"

Even when the accursed appendages had not yet made an appearance and Lux didn't seem aware of their existence within him, he asked.

"Why aren't you afraid of me? Why don't you hate me? Why aren't you being destroyed by me?"

Illiaz felt pieces in his mind fall out of place. The way the question was burned so deep in Lux's psyche that it persisted past the repetitious loss of his memories caused a scratching beneath the bones of Illiaz's ribs. "Why are you so afraid of destroying me, Lux?" Illiaz smiled because he wanted to laugh and knew that if he did it would be bloody. "Why are so you convinced that you're going to destroy me?"

His body was doing a fine job of destroying him all on its own.

"I destroy everybody."

Illiaz simpered, feeling that Lux somehow wasn't seeing it. "I thought you didn't remember anything."

"I…" The gladiator's lips pursed as he was befuddled and thrown off. "I don't remember."

His lips pursed further, parted uncertainly, tongue brushing over chapped flesh and his brow crinkling.

"Then how can you know that, Lux? That everyone is

destroyed by you."

"It's just a feeling."

"And because of this feeling you're afraid that you'll destroy me, too?"

He couldn't be destroyed when he'd never been whole.

But Lux looked utterly lost and confused. Luminous gold irises but white sclera veined with so much bloody red. Intricate spiderwebs of it.

"Yes...but also no. I simply don't understand how you haven't disintegrated yet. It's..." Lux's smile was small and squishy-soft, like a caterpillar. "No offense, but you look fragile. Yet you haven't broken, and you don't look like you're going to...like I said, I don't remember anything. I just have these vague feelings of the way things are, or were..."

Maybe that caterpillar-smile was poisonous or laced with spines; or maybe it was perfectly benign.

"There's not much in my head, to be honest, but what little is there doesn't line up..." A fluid, crawling shrug. "It's just disorienting, to an extent."

"And if you did destroy me simply by being around me?"

"Then I wouldn't know what to do. You're the only person who exists for me."

Maybe they were both stuck in this atrium. Unable to leave, only able to circle each other, observe each other, for there existed nothing else for either of them to do. There was no one else here.

"And that's the only reason why you care." Illiaz smiled, because he didn't have many options in life to make choice of; but whether or not to smile was one of the few. "Are you scared of being alone, Lux?"

"...No."

Lux was looking at him searchingly. It was a devastating look. Coruscations in Illiaz's gaze when he blinked.

"I just don't know what I'm supposed to do in this world. What my purpose is..."

Ah, of course. Lux had always lived in order to fulfill his sense of purpose. Now, having none...no wonder he was so lost.

"What is my purpose here, Illiaz?"

When Lux said his name, it made Illiaz shiver.

"—Why am I here?"

Illiaz understood why he was being asked. He was the only one from whom Lux could seek answers. But he didn't understand why he was expected to know.

Coruscations still in his gaze each time he blinked—and he couldn't keep himself from blinking, because his eyes stung terribly.

They'd brought Lux here because they'd believed that Illiaz could contain him. But why they'd believed that, and why he could indeed do so, were different matters entirely.

"...You're here because if I'm with you, you won't leave; and if you're with me, I won't kill myself."

By the deities, how *badly* he'd wanted to kill himself.

He couldn't help but laugh, covering his mouth with a hand to hide the blood that sprayed over his lips, palm, and fingers. He licked the coppery saltiness off; if he didn't, then Lux would.

He didn't understand how everything had come to this.

"For whatever reason, it seems the deities do not yet want our suffering to end. And so..." He spread his arms, curving his licked-clean lips into a smile. "Here we are. Tethered to each other by a thread of Fate that neither of us can comprehend."

Lux's eyelids lowered slightly, dubious, and Illiaz folded back in on himself with laughter that bubbled from his lungs. He choked on the blood that rose up into his mouth and throat with his dark mirth. He kept both of his hands, one over the other, pressed over his lips until he was able to swallow it all back down—the hysterics and the blood.

The pain made it hard to think: there were bright, blinding little flashes going off everywhere.

Sometimes, when he looked at Lux, he could place those flashes far away from him as stars in a bruise-blue night sky, and see that all the scintillations had colors. He could see them as being beautiful, like that.

Lux did not suffer pain, but rather accepted it as the night accepted shadows.

Illiaz was falling apart. Devouring and digesting himself from the inside with an utterly insensible hunger, subsisting primarily on the blood he choked up from his lungs. Eating and ingesting himself.

But Lux just looked at him, his gaze desperate and distraught. "If you're jealous of me, then why don't you hate me?"

Illiaz tried to process this through the flashes of pain. Distant like the stars.

"...But I'm not jealous of you, Lux." Why ever would he be jealous? "I could never be capable of being what you are—it would break me. But you're capable of being what you are without breaking. And I find that admirable. Inspiring, even."

Illiaz thought of silver thistle: like the night sky. But crawling over the ground.

He held Lux's butterfly-wing gaze, feeling his eyes prickle as if with thistle-thorns.

Lux was looking at him with a disbelief that was almost awe, almost fascination, almost amazement. Almost delight and almost happiness. "You don't want to be like me."

Illiaz smiled, silver thistles in his eyes and between his teeth. "No. I don't."

Lux looked utterly uncomprehending, and Illiaz felt the same, and it was somewhat comical.

Lux shook his head like a dog. He couldn't understand, and Illiaz couldn't understand why Lux couldn't understand, and Lux couldn't understand why he couldn't understand that he couldn't understand, and Lux was stepping closer with that expression that tickled his insides with fluttering wings like butterflies.

"Why?"

Lux was so close that Illiaz could feel his breath. It smelled of rotting flesh. The scent was familiar; comfortable.

"Because that would be painful, in its own way."

Lux's tongue ran hungrily over his bottom lip, no doubt enticed by the smell of blood, and Illiaz's expression softened.

"If I were like you, Lux, I'd also be closing my eyes and falling down stairs just to feel something. Your lack of feeling is both a blessing and a curse, just as my pain is."

The thick scent of rotting flesh was making Illiaz dizzy. Blood in his lungs and he felt like he was dying.

Blood in his lungs and a heart that, still alive, kept pumping it there.

Lux was still staring at him. "So then what do you want to be?"

Ah, Lux was giving him no space to breathe. No space to collect his thoughts. Crowding and overwhelming him like that. "What do I want to...be?"

Illiaz hummed, making sure it was musical, melodious, and harmonious like the intertwining scents of rotting flesh and fermenting blood. He blinked with glitter on his eyelashes, turned the throbs of agony in his body to a pleasant breeze, and moved with the weightless grace of smoke curling from a blown-out candle. He shifted his stance ever so slightly, more light and open at the shoulders and hips, weight perfectly balanced over his feet, energy in the movements of his arms as if the air were weighted like water; and he tilted his head and lifted his chin slightly to arc and open his neck.

It guided Lux's eyes away from his own long enough for him to think, and he smiled, a warmer and less empty smile than before.

"By virtue of your being what I'm not capable of being, you make me glad to be myself, Lux."

Lux's gaze crawled over him like spider legs till it made its way back to his eyes. He stared at Illiaz for a long moment and then abruptly took a step back, shaking his head as if he'd been caught in cobwebs and was trying to dislodge the strands.

"...No, I don't understand. I give up. You're incomprehensible."

A roll of those bronze shoulders, the muscles of his pectorals and abdominals hard and defined as the platings of a scorpion, skin crawling with the myriad accursed appendages beneath. It was why there wasn't much point in Lux wearing a shirt: the arachnoid appendages just tore through. As such he wore only his loose black pants. The only gold on him now was the threads woven into his sandals, and the iridescence of the shiny black appendages whenever they broke through his skin—as they did now, large scorpion legs and stinger tearing out from his back and waving in the air behind him. Lux didn't appear to notice.

Illiaz smiled at him. "As we all are incomprehensible to each other, for we can never be any way other than the way we are."

One of the arachnoid legs tickled Lux's face, and he brushed it away with a hand, keeping his gaze on Illiaz. "There is clearly no rhyme or reason to the world."

It made Illiaz laugh. Blood in his mouth and he didn't even care. "I don't disagree, but what a way for you to come to that conclusion."

Lux was regarding him perplexedly, twitching slightly as the accursed appendages dug themselves into the skin of his shoulders. He hit them away again and they retreated, disappearing behind his back, followed by the soft sound of spiderweb strands drawn through flesh behind them.

All that, and Lux was still looking at him in bafflement.

Lux would almost certainly lose control again. And even if that, by some miracle, didn't happen, the accursed gladiator's memory would remain spotty. He forgot things even when he didn't lose all his memories from having sustained new brain damage.

It made Illiaz want to sob, but he no longer had the energy.

Lux was soon going to lose his memory, and Illiaz was soon going to die. Was it enough to have this, for just a brief moment? Whatever he and Lux were getting out of this was nothing that either of them could keep.

Illiaz was dizzy, scintillating constellations of pain whirling around him. He would have fallen, but Lux held him up. Illiaz wondered if it was because Lux ate dead bodies that he was so willing to embrace a corpse.

Lux's butterfly-wing eyes fluttered closed and a cicada-like hum vibrated his chest. Illiaz wondered idly what Lux's accursed appendages would feel like tearing into his flesh. It made Illiaz chuckle. Lux must have been able to tell that something was amiss, because he pulled away, looking at him with those firebug-carapace eyes. Illiaz smirked back at him, aching and empty.

There was no warmth in his body, and he didn't want this. He didn't mind if Lux ate him—dead bodies were meant to be eaten—but he didn't want Lux showing affection to a carcass.

"Close your eyes, Luxanthus."

Lux closed his eyes.

"Let me go, Luxanthus."

Lux let him go.

"Stay perfectly still, Luxanthus."

Lux stayed perfectly still, hardly even moving to breathe.

Illiaz was exhausted, aching, weak, trembling as he crossed over to the dark curtains, thin slivers of sunlight on the floor and wall at their edges. His hand on the thick fabric, Illiaz's voice cracked with emotion. "You know, Lux. I might actually be a monster."

Lux remained perfectly still where he was, and his voice was smooth and serene. "So am I, Illiaz."

"...So you are." It made Illiaz smile, aching and empty. "In that case, Lux, I won't tell you that I'm sorry for this."

He pulled open the curtains, letting the sunlight in. The golden rays fell over Lux and the accursed gladiator went rigid first and then a second later screamed, falling to his knees on the floor with his head in his hands, giant arachnoid appendages bursting out of his flesh and flailing wildly in the air, smashing into the ceiling, the walls, the ground.

What one didn't remember couldn't hurt them, and Illiaz was dying, almost dead. Soon, he would no longer exist, and all this pain he was suffering would be meaningless.

What one didn't remember couldn't hurt them, and he wanted

Lux to forget. Presently all this pain Lux was suffering would no longer exist. He'd forget that he'd embraced Illiaz and the topic of their conversation. He'd forget that Illiaz had opened the curtains and made him scream and writhe. He'd forget about the anti-Accursed unit fighting off his myriad accursed appendages and impaling him through his skull.

Illiaz laughed like little silver wind-chimes echoing around an empty graveyard. "Love really is terribly cruel, isn't it?"

Was there anything more selfish than wanting someone else to exist for one's own sake? To love someone was to want something from them, whether or not they wanted to give it. And Illiaz smiled, utterly empty except for this agonizing, coruscating pain that told him he was alive.

Only the living had the privilege of hurting.

He fought through the pain to watch as the anti-Accursed unit streamed in; he'd already closed the curtains, by then. They'd never know that this time he'd caused the accursed gladiator's breakdown by intention.

And when Lux woke up without his memories after healing from a blade shoved through his skull, Illiaz chose once again to upkeep his perfect, beautiful illusion, his fantastical act. This time he wouldn't let himself fall. What else could he do? Even caring for Lux like this was a choice—to keep him near but to hold him at a distance, because Lux was his reason for keeping himself alive but he didn't want to be Lux's reason for living. Not when he would so soon no longer exist. Better that Lux be lost and meaningless from the beginning of his memory and until he found a reason for existing that would last, than to hinge his existence on Illiaz only to lose him.

Illiaz was going to die. It turned out that he did not want Lux to care.

Illiaz's life had never been his own, so *by all the deities,* he wanted, at the very least, for his death to be his and his alone. He did not want any part of his death to belong to Lux.

He'd always hated it when people saw his pain and were hurt by it, because that pain was all his existence *was,* and it should have been *his.* They shouldn't have been allowed to make his pain *theirs.*

Letting his heavy head fall back against the wall, he looked up at the ornately carved ceiling, the murals painted there that he usually forgot existed and even now wasn't really seeing. He'd long ago stopped wondering why the deities were so cruel, for there would be times he would wake from an utterly dreamless sleep, and feel he understood: how maddening it was to truly feel nothing at all.

Illiaz was so tired, now, but he could not sleep. If he slept, he would never wake up again. So he couldn't sleep. Couldn't allow himself to sleep.

But he was so tired, and he couldn't muster up the energy or motivation to get his excruciating body to move until Lux began to stir, and Illiaz knew the accursed gladiator would soon awaken.

If he wanted to appear to be beautiful and perfect, it was necessary that he collect himself.

Out of desirous necessity, he contracted his weak and agonizing muscles and pulled himself together, pushed himself up to his feet, crossed over to a corner table where there was a bouquet of flowers. He pulled out a rose with his fingers, tore away the petals with his teeth, chewed their acrid bitterness deliberately and swallowed.

Lux was stirring, and Illiaz crossed over to him, graceful and light as if nothing instead of everything hurt him. He brushed his fingers gently through the accursed gladiator's hair.

Lux's butterfly-wing eyes opened and caught vaguely on his face, and Illiaz curved his lips softly.

It had been a summer afternoon when Illiaz had asked him; Lux had just finished training in the dirt arena of the horse corral, and he'd walked over to where Illiaz had been watching, perched sitting on the fence. Lux had been resplendent and shining with all his gold adornments and all his drips and trails of sweat catching the sunlight so brightly he was almost blinding: cracks of lightning and crackles of stars in his skin, scintillations of sun. Bronze and tiger's eye glimmering, like he wasn't even alive, but something immortal and divine.

It had made Illiaz smile at him, feeling such a hollow aching inside the cage of his ribs. As if his heart were missing from his chest.

"Say, Lux. What is it that makes you feel alive?"

"Hm?"

Those luminous gold eyes on him like suns themselves, and Illiaz had smiled like a flower the sunlight had tickled into bloom.

"What makes you feel the most alive? Is it fighting?"

Those eyes sun-blank on him, and the blossom of Illiaz's smile had opened its petals wider, as if to catch even more of that light.

"—Or is it something else?"

Lux had blinked, looking up at the sky.

"What makes me feel the most alive...? It's not fighting. Fighting is like dreaming; it's instinct, and it's effortless. I don't have to think about it. What makes me feel the most alive is...making decisions, I suppose. Conscious choices that determine the course of my life."

Lux's voice had dragged claw-scars down to Illiaz's core, hot-cold in his bones.

"—Feeling like, out of all the possible paths which I could walk, I am determinedly choosing the one that I want to walk best."

The flower of Illiaz's smile bloomed ever further as those gold-sun eyes again shone their light upon him.

"I see."

"Most people in my life have broken around me, without any action or intention of my own. You're not like that, though. And so I have the feeling with you that I...can choose exactly what I want to be to you."

Lux had grinned at him. In Illiaz's mind, the expression had called up memories of desserts sticky with cinnamon and honey, of brazen midday rays glowing on dunes of golden sands for as far as the eye could see.

A soft, aromatic feeling had settled inside Illiaz, like quiet sprays of rose-and-sandalwood perfume. A curl to his lips like the petals of a wild rose bloom.

But that had been then; he'd only meant anything to Lux in the context of Lux's former life. Had only meant something to him as being different from all those who had been broken throwing themselves against him. To a Lux without memories of all those people who had broken, the fact that Illiaz wasn't breaking meant nothing.

It was droll, actually: Illiaz felt a little bit like he *was* breaking, now.

Lux's eyes blank on him like butterfly wings and Illiaz could do nothing but smile, like an inviting flower.

In the end, Illiaz was too weak to break. He wasn't hard enough to crack and snap—he simply bent and decayed, softly and without sound.

It had been late that summer afternoon when Lux had asked him; Illiaz light on the ground like a bird, all hollow bones and flight-suggestive feathers, and Lux with sunlit trails of sweat like molten cracks in his bronze skin.

"What about you?"

Illiaz had blinked at him and fought the urge to shield his eyes from that sun-burning gaze.

"Me?"

The curve of those lips had made flowers look listless. "What makes you feel the most alive, Illiaz?"

Illiaz, looking at him—Lux all aglow in gold and sun-bright sweat—had hardly been able to breathe; when he had exhaled, it had been weak and shaky.

"Beauty. Witnessing beauty makes me feel alive."

When he'd simpered, the expression had been a death-defying thing, like the first blooms daring winter not to give way to spring.

Those golden eyes on him, unremitting. "Out of all the gladiators you could have housed...why me?"

The question had been far more incredulous than curious, and it had made Illiaz want to laugh.

As if it could ever have been anyone but Lux.

"Why you?" Illiaz had smiled. "I suppose it's because I feel that we're similar."

He'd had Lux's riveted attention, and so he'd relaxed his expression slightly, made it softer, more accepting, like a rose being made both to glimmer and to weaken beneath all the raindrops hitting it.

"The fact that I'm a piece of decoration and you're a weapon makes this relationship uncomplicated. We don't have to deal with any expectations for any kind of a relationship. We can simply, dissociate as unrelated objects."

Lux had regarded him for a moment, visage impassive and eyes as dispassionate as suns. Then his mouth had cracked into a grin and he'd chuckled, looking down in a way that made his luminous-dark hair fall into his eyes. The grin had tugged at his lips.

"Heh. I suppose neither of us wants all that much, do we? To engage with someone without breaking them; to be, for once, the one to gaze instead of the one always only being gazed at."

It had made Illiaz laugh slightly in return, a feeling of petals tickling behind his eyes.

Illiaz, in pain and dying as he was, didn't have the energy to put into a complicated relationship that wouldn't even last; and Lux, empty of hunger as he was, never did anything except that which was the most strategic action in any given circumstance. Neither of them had the desire or will to put in the effort to maintain anything involved.

And yet they both had still craved some kind of connection. It wouldn't have worked, otherwise.

Lux had raised his head again and looked at Illiaz with that bright smile and those shining eyes. "I guess we both wanted something just like this."

Illiaz's own lips had curved in return. "I suppose we did."

But that had been before, when he had meant something to Lux in the context of the rest of Lux's life, and Lux had been someone who had understood him because they were similar in the kinds of roles they so consciously fulfilled. What were they to each other now? Fellow prisoners and jailors in that place, both keeping the other there.

"Are you to me what you want to be?"

What were they to each other now? Was he to Lux what he wanted to be to him? It didn't matter, really.

"I'm in your life, aren't I?"

When Illiaz had asked Lux again it had been midday, but all the curtains were drawn closed, and inside the mansion it was forever dark and candlelit. Lux had been lying at the bottom of a flight of steps staring dazedly up at the ceiling while Illiaz had stood over him and looked down, forever failing to meet that distant-staring gaze.

"Say, Lux."

"Hm?"

Lux had stirred slightly, but still didn't flutter his butterfly-wing gaze to the wide-open flowers of Illiaz's eyes.

"What is it that makes you feel alive?"

A blinking of eyelashes, or a fluttering of wings—did it matter? Arachnoid curses beneath Lux's skin crawling like drips of sweat had once traced over his flesh in the sun.

"I...don't know. I don't know if I even do feel alive."

There was a feeling in Illiaz's chest like drips of candlewax, and he'd looked up at the ceiling. As if the darkness there would be balm to any of his pain. Maybe to the brightness of it.

"...I see."

"What about you?"

It had surprised Illiaz, a little, even though it probably shouldn't have, and when he'd looked back down at Lux lying there on the floor without a single injury on him, the accursed gladiator had finally met his gaze.

As if Illiaz could have responded in any other way but to smile. "Beauty, Lux. Witnessing beauty makes me feel alive."

Lux blinked up at him. "I don't understand."

"You wouldn't, no."

Lux had been lying languidly dazed on the stone-tile floor, at the bottom of a flight of steps he'd tumbled down because he'd been sprinting laughingly down hallways with his eyes tightly closed while leaking tears had sparkled in the candlelight and glowed gold-orange behind him, like drops of sun.

Now, Lux's eyes were dry, looking up at Illiaz unreadably and with far more elegance than bloodshot eyes had any right to.

A slight pull of a frown to Lux's lips—and it was a despondent look on him, like a spiderweb that had once been lustrous and sinuous, collecting dust and sagging.

"So if all I feel is emptiness, as if this is nothing but a dream..."

Illiaz hummed, remembering the way that, even as screams had echoed from the city of Mythus as it had been overrun by Accursed, Lux, about to enter into it, had curved his lips, almost smirking. "Then I imagine it would be a feeling of consciousness that would make you feel alive, Lux."

"A feeling of consciousness?"

Lux looked at him, and Illiaz smiled with the salty-savory copper tang of blood and the sweet-feigning bitterness of roses on his teeth. "A feeling that you are not just dreaming but are making decisions and choosing for yourself. What makes us feel the most alive is the counterweight to what makes us feel the most dead, is it not?"

Lux, lying supine on the floor, looking up at him torpidly, tilted his head.

"Pain makes you feel dead?"

The world spun. Illiaz fixed his smile as if, by doing so, he could hold it all in place.

"Does your emptiness not make you think it might be better to be dead, Lux?"

Lux looked up at him, blank as stone, before turning away as if Illiaz's gaze were making him feel nauseous. "...No, you're right:

sometimes I do think that."

Another day, and Lux was curled on the bed, his eyes closed in sleep; but he kept twitching, various expressions fleeting over his face. Nothing particularly distinctive, but certainly a larger variety than graced his features when he was awake. Illiaz watched him.

He himself didn't sleep, not anymore. Sometimes he lay beside Lux while the accursed gladiator slept, watching him; sometimes he lay beside Lux while the accursed gladiator slept, but turned away from him; sometimes he just wandered around the room, rearranging, cleaning, or observing Lux from a distance.

Lux's twitching was turning to writhing, and Illiaz walked over to wake him. Lux was in one of his incarnations in which he was unaware of the insect appendages inside him, and Illiaz had learned that when they made their appearance due to his troubled dreams and he awoke with them broken out of his skin, things went unpleasantly.

So he walked over, reaching out with a hand, preparing to wake the accursed gladiator.

Illiaz doubted that Lux, despite the agitated movement, was scared or disturbed within his dreams. Probably he was just trying to fight, in that natural, effortless way he did while awake, but the unconscious state of his body was partially restraining him.

In Illiaz's dreams, back when he used to sleep, his mother had wrapped her corpse-cold arms around him, whispered for him to smile, and then fell into an abyss of darkness, taking him with her.

Illiaz wouldn't ever sleep again. Not until he was dead.

Lux was the reason he still wanted to be alive, and it hurt him so terribly he almost wished that the gladiator didn't exist. If Lux didn't exist, then he'd be able to finally just give up and stop fighting, stop struggling, stop suffering. It made Illiaz laugh helplessly, every shake racking him with agony and yet he couldn't stop.

"Do you need a glass of water?"

Lux's tone as he asked was so utterly *confused,* and that caused Illiaz's laughter to wrench itself violently and horrifically free from his chest. Blood coughed up into his mouth and Illiaz, in a panic, desperately covered his mouth with both hands.

It wouldn't be enough to prevent the blood from leaking through, he knew, but he didn't want to let Lux see; and so what strength he had he used to throw his body from the bed onto the floor, knowing that Lux wouldn't care enough to follow him.

In the darkness pooled on the floor, barely penetrated by the candlelight from the table, maybe the blood could be passed off as a trick of the shadows. Maybe the scent wouldn't be detectable over that of burning beeswax, of the perfume-aroma of roses and sandalwood.

Desperate thoughts tried to push through the blinding waves of his agony, like flies trying to make it through the minuscule gaps in a finely woven spiderweb only to get caught in the strands, wrapped all up in it until they were no longer distinguishable, were melted to formlessness and devoured by the spider that made its home there.

Maybe the agony lasted for seconds, maybe minutes, maybe hours—it felt like an eternity. But it finally did subside. Illiaz came slowly back to himself, becoming aware of the taste of all the blood in his mouth, the feeling of it on his hands. The wet gasping sounds of his breaths, the heave of his ribs, the darkness in his eyes. The fear of death growing in his mind like the shadows cast by a sinking sun.

When he finally managed to gather up his meager strength—he felt so *weak,* so *heavy*—and push himself up to a sitting position, looking back over at the bed, Lux was lying there with his eyes closed and breathing evenly, seeming to be in sleep.

Illiaz was covered in blood—the lower half of his face, his neck, his shirt, his hands, his arms. He carefully, painfully pushed himself up to his feet, walked swayingly to the bathroom, closed and locked the door. He went about stripping himself, washing his body, redoing his makeup. He had to go back into the room for clean clothes, but fortunately Lux was still asleep. Illiaz had suspected it, from the sound of thrashing, which Lux only did when in the clutches of dreams.

When Illiaz stepped out, Lux was curled up and biting chunks out of the flesh of his hand, getting blood all over the bed even as the arachnoid appendages burst from his flesh, healing him almost as quickly as he was eating himself. Illiaz blinked at him, feeling deathly tired. He crossed unsteadily to the dresser and redressed himself before turning and crossing over to the bed. He used the short distance to gather himself, dragging up the energy to bring ease and grace to his movements, alarm and concern to his expression.

He took Lux's chewed-up hand in his own and threw his entire bodyweight into the action of trying to pull it away from Lux's teeth. It used up almost all the rest of his energy to muster up a tone of urgency.

"Lux! Lux, stop! Stop it!"

Lux's eyes flew open, the whites and irises of his eyes completely dark red with blood, his pupils like the darkest voids at their centers. An inverted lunar eclipse.

Those eyes fixed on Illiaz's face. "What?"

Lux's voice was disoriented and slightly wet with his blood, and Illiaz kept his hands carefully covering the small arachnoid appendages that were finishing repairing the damaged flesh of Lux's hand.

Illiaz looked away, both so the movement would attract and hold Lux's gaze and so that he didn't have to expend as much energy manipulating his expression. If it went lax, Lux wouldn't see it, and turning his face away would be indication enough of distress. And he could sound like he was disturbed simply by letting his voice go quiet and speaking slowly, further sparing his drained energy.

"You had a nightmare again."

These occurrences had become so normal that Illiaz wasn't even fazed. The only bothersome part was that there was blood on the bed, and he'd have to change the covers. He was already so drained, and his entire body ached, throbbed, and stung.

Still, Lux was striking there, the golden light of flame dancing over him, the dark shimmering of his hair, the blood covering his hand and filling his eyes, the steam of his warm breath he exhaled softly into the cold air. "Oh."

He made Illiaz want so desperately to live forever.

"It's not your fault, Lux."

It was never Lux's fault, the things that other people felt or did to themselves because of him. The gladiator didn't intentionally construct his comportment the way Illiaz did. Lux was simply naturally, effortlessly flawless. In everything he did and said, in every situation he found himself in.

Such a perfection as Lux's was a terrifying thing: the way it made Illiaz want to keep living even despite the agony he could feel driving his mind to the most distant edges of sanity.

Lux's red eyes were glancing over the blood that was smeared over his skin and the bed, a slight furrow in his brow and a pursing to his lips.

"Did I do this?"

He looked at Illiaz, meeting his gaze searchingly. The blood was slowly draining out of his eyes, and soon the golden color of his irises would return, with the crimson nothing more than spider-webbing lines.

Illiaz felt so heavy, like he'd crumple beneath the weight of the air. Desperately trying to hold himself together, he imagined himself a bird, a peacock or a golden pheasant—a creature with hollow bones and resplendent feathers. He could force himself to shrug just that lightly, could force himself to smile just that brightly.

"Well, *I* didn't do it."

Illiaz hadn't realized that his hair had been dripping water until drops fell onto Lux's face, Lux shivering and then reaching up to dry them. His expression was mildly disquieted.

"I'm sorry."

Illiaz shook his head, and Lux winced slightly at the drops of water that fell from him. Illiaz wondered if they were cold. Over his deathly skin, even cold water felt warm. Lux's skin burned him.

"Like I said, Lux, it's not your fault."

He took Lux's hand and took a step back, making it clear that his intent was to pull Lux from the bed. Lux stood up easily. Illiaz smiled at him, as elegantly as he could, hoping to keep Lux's gaze focused on him so the accursed gladiator wouldn't see just how much blood there was and realize that some of it had been not from him but from Illiaz's laughter. "Don't worry. I'll clean it."

However he'd smiled apparently wasn't distraction enough, because Lux glanced back and his eyes widened slightly at the extent of darkening, congealing blood. He looked back at Illiaz, and his gaze was far too lucid. "I can help."

If he did, Illiaz wouldn't be able to hide the weakness in his limbs, the pain lancing through him, the shreds of lung on the carpet.

It was all he could do to keep his movements light and graceful, his tone light and airy, his expression light and easy.

"Don't worry about it, Lux. I'd prefer to do it myself. You go clean yourself."

There was a mental retreat in Lux's gaze, a mental shuttering. Lux's shoulders slumped ever so minutely. His chin lowered slightly, soft strands of dark hair in his face stirring with his breath. "I'm sorry."

Lux, even without his memories, had the psyche of someone who was used to carrying burdens, not causing them. And certainly not leaving them to others.

Lux's eyes through his hair were blank and unreadable, distant.

The expression of complete defeat didn't suit him, and Illiaz found himself putting all his effort into smiling charmingly, laughing easily, making himself seem light and carefree like gently breeze-danced silver bells and soft moonlight.

"No, no, it's not that, Lux. It's just that nobody else can ever clean anything to my satisfaction. It's a lot easier to just clean things myself."

A carefully chosen half-truth—he'd long ago realized that others did not share his acute attention to detail, his painful need for perfection. For as long as he could remember, he'd found himself cleaning rooms that the servants had just cleaned, getting all the spots they'd missed, overlooked, or simply hadn't cared about, but that had been to him like burrs against his skin.

Illiaz could see the way Lux's eyes slid back into focus. He felt a sudden sense of dread as Lux blinked, shifting his eyes to look at him, scarlet-webbed gaze far too lucid.

"There've been spiderwebs in the mansion, recently."

His tone was in no way accusatory—it was nothing but a simple, curious statement of fact—but it was like ice in Illiaz's veins. As if he hadn't already felt cold as the dead. Now he was even colder.

"...I must have missed those."

Curse the servants and their lack of attention to detail. He hadn't been able to check the mansion for spiders and insects, recently; he'd been growing weaker and weaker, his illness eating him alive from the inside and his death's murmurings increasing to a scream in his bones. The bruises from internal bleeding blooming like roses of starless night sky over his sickly pale skin. The uncontrollable atrophying of what little muscle he'd managed to build up.

Lux was looking at him with those eyes like the iridescent wings of butterflies, his voice the gentlest stirrings of air. "It doesn't bother me."

It was all Illiaz could do just to smile. "No, I imagine it wouldn't."

Lux had looked utterly content and calm with the spiders crawling over him.

Illiaz had to force his weak muscles to hold his bones without shaking as Lux looked at him with a gaze far too lucid for its lurid lightning-fissures of broken veins.

"Does it bother you that much? The suits of armor are also all damaged; the statues are missing their heads...that doesn't bother you?"

Illiaz's weak laughter, at the very least, gave him an excuse to let his body shake. "They're clean, aren't they? I don't mind if things are broken. It's only when they're dirty that it bothers me."

Sometimes things that were broken were more beautiful than they'd been whole, like shattered glass that glittered dazzlingly. Things that were dirty with neglect, though, were always ugly: those obvious signs of degradation. The acute reminder that everything that existed would have its end.

Lux's eyes, dark as they were with webbing lines of blood, should not be so bright in dim gold flickerings of candlelight.

"Then you don't mind that I keep having nightmares—just the blood that gets everywhere."

There was blood in Illiaz's mouth as he laughed, hidden by curling in on himself slightly, head lowered and white hair obscuring his face until he could swallow it all down, swipe his tongue over his teeth to make sure there would be no red when he looked back up. He brushed a hand back through his hair to attract Lux's eyes so he might not see any blood he had missed. "I suppose so."

Illiaz couldn't help but look from the darkening crimson on Lux's skin to that on the bed, on the carpet. If it had the chance to dry, it would be significantly harder to clean. It was all he could do not to grit his teeth. All he could do to keep his gaze from swimming.

By the *deities*, it was already going to be difficult enough, with how terribly weak he was.

Lux's gaze had followed his, bafflement flickering with the candlelight over his features. "How did I manage to do that, anyway?" He lifted his bloodied arm, examining it, his brow furrowing slightly and tongue flicking over the carmine flecks still decorating his lip. "My skin is bloody, but it isn't broken."

His far-too-lucid gaze shifted from his arm to Illiaz's face and then over his body, those butterfly eyes narrowing slightly, his tone flattening. "Are you sure it's mine?"

If he was examining Illiaz for concealed injuries he wasn't going to find any, and Illiaz made a scoffing exhale through his nose.

"Well, it's not mine, and it's not anyone else's." He turned toward the bed and waved a hand at Lux dismissively, his impatience growing to near panic; it was becoming so, so difficult to keep his body from trembling, his balance from wavering. "Go wash yourself while I take care of this, Lux."

"Do I know other people aside from you, Illiaz?"

Illiaz cursed Lux's incisive mind even as he delighted in it. Still, if this was a game of jabbing questions and dodging answers, then Illiaz was going to win. Lux didn't have the psyche of someone who had ever had to manipulate others' perceptions of him. Lux had always been so strong that he could simply carry whatever was given to him—and that was always what he'd done, without seeking anything more.

Illiaz, though, was someone who'd always had to hide his pain and true nature from those around him. Lux would not catch him because Lux neither knew how nor had the drive to try.

Yet it was all Illiaz could do just to keep himself standing, pain lancing through him and the world wavering, vivid sparks leaping up from roaring flames and burning to ash to drift like dirty gray snowflakes in the night.

Lux was looking at him, and Illiaz blinked back, the ground disappearing from beneath his feet. "What?" An echo of what Lux had asked after waking up from a distressing dream.

Lux gestured toward Illiaz's mouth, tilting his head slightly. Dark bangs shadowed his face, but his eyes behind them were far too bright and lucid.

"You've got blood on you, too, you know."

Illiaz became suddenly aware of the hot mass of salty blood in his mouth, the dripping of it down his chin.

He knew that his eyes went too wide, knew that his hands flew to his mouth too fast, knew that trying to cover it up now was useless. He knew, too, that he couldn't stop it now, knew it viscerally as the uncontrollable hacking coughs racked his chest. Still, he covered his mouth desperately, *uselessly* with his hands, because giving up would be far, far worse. To neglect to try was a far more loathsome fate than to try his hardest and fail.

He could feel Lux's eyes on him, but he couldn't bring himself to meet that lucid, lurid gaze.

"You're bleeding, Illiaz."

Lux said it so flatly.

"—Did I do that?"

Illiaz shook his head vehemently, denied it truthfully, prayed desperately to any of the deities that happened to be listening that Lux would believe him.

The deities' laughter rang in his ears along with Lux's low voice.

"—You wouldn't lie to me about that, would you, Illiaz?"

"No."

At the very least Illiaz had managed to remember to place dark handkerchiefs in the pockets of his loose pants, so he had something to press over his mouth to hide and absorb the blood. The only problem was that it made his voice indistinct, muffled, dubious. He pulled the cloth from his mouth, carefully imbuing his voice with all the strength and authority he could muster. He prayed desperately to the laughing deities that Lux would believe him as he said: "It's fine."

It was too late, at this point. Still he was desperate and panicking. He didn't—

By the deities, he *didn't*—

He knew that he was dying, knew that he was almost dead, knew that he didn't have more than a few hours—the grinning of his death behind his lips all the way up his cheeks—but he didn't—

He didn't want to die as ugly and pathetic as *this*. He wanted—

He wanted—

Lux exhaled, slow and resigned. A current on the ocean carrying Illiaz like a boat far out to sea beyond the sight of land, stranding him there.

"Well, you're not going to tell me anything that you don't want me to know. Go ahead and carry whatever you feel like carrying."

Illiaz didn't think anyone else could ever or would ever sound so disappointed as Lux at not being burdened with something.

There were only a couple of gold-plated metal bangles around Lux's wrist, the ones that the chains attached to, but they glimmered luminously in the candlelight when he waved his hand, unbelievably bright against the dark of the dried blood on his skin.

"If you don't want to weigh me down with it, Illiaz, then you can weigh me down with gold."

Lux's gaze settling on the chains Illiaz had removed and set on the bedside table, his expression like impenetrable fog.

Did Lux remember, somewhere in the back of his mind, that he used to cover himself with gold adornments? That he used to try to weigh himself down with them, since otherwise everything was far too easy?

"—I suppose there are the chains, too."

It was all Illiaz could do not to choke on his own blood. He gasped out weakly, despairingly, *"I'm sorry."*

Illiaz wasn't entirely sure exactly what he was apologizing for. Everything, maybe. He didn't know. Everything was agonizing. It was hard to think, and he wished Lux would leave the room so he could let himself sag against the bed. Or the wall. Or the floor. Just a few moments to gather his strength. To swallow the masses of blood and lung-flesh that he couldn't stop coughing into his mouth.

"It's fine. It doesn't bother me any."

Lux was being dismissive, but Illiaz had known him long enough by now—had known so many different iterations of him by now—that he could tell the accursed gladiator was vexed.

Illiaz's lips were hidden behind the dark handkerchief, unable to be seen, but for some reason he still smiled. Probably it was just automatic reflex, at that point. "Which part?"

"All of it." Lux shrugged with the graceful ease that came entirely from strength. His gaze on Illiaz was dull of emotion but challenging in its intensity. "None of it bothers me. I don't know if this is because I don't remember anything, but I don't really feel anything."

The blood had finally stopped rising into Illiaz's mouth, so he pulled the dark handkerchief from his lips and curved them artfully.

It was his most beautiful smile, the one that had him imagining fields of flowers swaying harmoniously in the breeze and paths of stars stretching bright and glittering across the night sky. "No, you've always been like that, Lux."

Lux's eyes met his, startled like fireflies that hadn't realized they could glow. "So you knew?"

He sounded surprised and disbelieving, and that made Illiaz want to laugh—except that if he did, he'd cough up more blood. Again. So he shoved the urge beneath the dark waters in his chest so that it gasped bubbles as it drowned.

Those bubbles rose to the surface and burst as a smile on his face, delicate. "I've always known."

Lux looked at him blankly, disbelievingly, gaze like butterfly eyespots. Vivid but flat and unblinking.

"So you care for me despite that? Or because of it?"

"Both." Illiaz felt so close to falling down and passing out. But still he smiled, because he could not allow himself to fall. "Go wash yourself already, Lux."

Lux blinked at him, his eyes widening ever so slightly in the way they always did when he remembered something he realized he'd forgotten. "Right."

His butterfly eyes swooped up to the ceiling, glided back down to rest ticklingly on Illiaz's face. "I forgot. And probably not for the first time, I take it?"

His gaze on Illiaz's was painfully searching.

Illiaz smiled at him tiredly. "You claim not to care about anything, Lux, but you're always asking questions."

Lux held his gaze for a long moment and then looked away, up at the dark ceiling that drizzled its shadows into his eyes like an hourglass drizzled sand. "I suppose so. I guess I am still curious."

A fluid shrug of Lux's muscular shoulders, gilt with candlelight and traced by shadows. "It occurs to me to ask, but then it doesn't occur to me to care when I don't receive answers. Whatever that means."

The dried blood was flaking from Lux's skin and descending in light drifts of dark dust, like scrapings of rust from metal. "I really don't know anything."

It sounded like an excuse, and it made Illiaz want to laugh cruelly. It was both so like and unlike Lux to bow out in that way; just like him to accept things as they were without trying to change them, but so unlike him to make such excuses for himself.

Then again, he didn't have any memories. How could Illiaz blame him for his ambivalence?

Illiaz made sure his voice was warm and light, like a spring breeze carrying with it the aroma of sunlit blossoms, playful and harmless. "Life is funny, huh?"

"I wouldn't know."

Lux was looking down, dark eyelashes obscuring his gaze, his tone a resigned descent of ash after a volcanic eruption, drifting down through cold air to settle on the ground where Illiaz's laughter tossed them up like a child scuffing its shoes, careless of the danger.

"No, I suppose you wouldn't." Illiaz was going to fall any second, now. Suffocate on air he could no longer breathe.

Lux wasn't looking at him but down at his hand, the dried blood flaking like tephra from his flesh. "I should go wash myself before I forget again."

"You should."

Lux moved with the easy grace of a shadow. Hardly had the door to the washroom clicked closed when Illiaz sagged against the bed, muscles spasming.

Ah, but there was blood drying in the duvet and the carpet. And Lux had asked to be weighed down. Illiaz didn't have the time to rest. If he allowed himself to close his eyes, he'd never open them again.

He pushed himself off the bed to his feet. He rolled up the carpet, first, opened the doors to the balcony and let the carpet fall outside. It would have to be dealt with later. Probably after he was already dead. He closed the doors again, drew shut the curtains.

There were more rugs rolled up in the closet, and he pulled one out, let it unroll itself over the floor. He crossed back over to the bed, knelt down at the base of it. He dragged out the woven baskets full of Lux's jewelry, pulled them to the middle of the floor, and left them there. Then he stripped the bloodied duvet off the bed, shoving it into the laundry hamper. He probably wouldn't live to see it cleaned. He pulled out new sheets, spreading them over the mattress. His entire body was trembling. Agony made it hard to see. He fell against the wall, losing the ability to support himself. He let himself relax there for a moment, but he didn't dare close his eyes.

Lux would be out of the washroom any minute. Illiaz could not afford to be found like this, slumped weakly and pathetically against the wall by the door. He imagined, again, his pain like stars decorating the night sky, imagined his weakness like rose-and-sandalwood perfume coating his skin, making his movements nothing but more meaningful, more alluring, more confident.

The clean duvet was on the bed but askew and crinkled. That wouldn't do. Illiaz carefully tugged it straight, meticulously smoothing the surface with a hand. He carefully didn't look over when he heard the washroom door open and saw the shadowy movement of Lux in the corner of his eye.

"...Are you sure you don't have any more gold?"

There was irony in Lux's voice, a soft metallic clinking as he picked up pieces of the jewelry and let them fall slowly back onto the pile, as if he couldn't believe that there was so much.

Illiaz let out a soft huff of air through his nose, feeling grateful he wasn't yet bleeding from there. "You asked for it, Lux. Did you not say you wanted to be weighed down with it?"

Lux gave a huff of his own, the sound warm and amused. "So I did."

The tone in Lux's voice was almost fond, and Illiaz clenched his eyes shut against the sudden sting, only to quickly open them again because the comfort of the darkness was terrifying.

He heard Lux going through the jewelry behind him, and as he listened, he finished smoothing out the duvet. He laid his painful body down on the bed, rolling carefully over to watch as Lux began donning the jewelry, starting with the largest pieces: the lavishly ornamented girdle that slung around his waist, hung with heavy gold pieces in round sun designs inset with deep-sky-blue lapis lazuli; the collar that stretched from breast to collarbone, woven densely with beads of gold, copper, lapis lazuli, green-blue faience, orange-red carnelian, and black obsidian. Lux moved from there to the chains strung with glittering gold circles—which he secured either around his waist or neck—to the necklaces hung with pendants, from simple gold bars and gemstones to intricate designs of scarab beetles, tigers, jackals, antelopes, and winged birds. He then moved to the gold armbands, and then to the bracelets and anklets, finishing by lining his fingers with rings and hanging what had always been his favorite pair of earrings in his ears.

Before Lux had lost his memories, he would carefully select different jewelry to wear each day, coordinating the colors and designs. Now, he simply donned every piece available.

When he was done, he was a glittering chaos of gold and colorful stones, shimmering with every movement like Illiaz's agony shimmered in his vision.

The weight of all that gold had to be incredible, but when Lux jumped, it was with lightness and ease. When he kicked, struck the air, performed flips and handsprings around the room as if in sparring practice, his movements were unobstructed by the jewelry, fluid and so fast that not even the loose pendants fell off when he was upside down. In the candlelight, the gold and gemstones glimmered like sunlight, like water, like fire.

Even weighed down with all that gold, Lux still looked far lighter than Illiaz with just his meager flesh and bones, the delicate, thin fabric of his clothes.

Illiaz's breath stole away for blissful moments—and then returned, painfully.

The accursed gladiator's expression was disappointed. "It's

terribly light."

Lux had always said he wanted to be weighed down. Illiaz smiled, because he knew that Lux had absolutely no idea what it was like to have to fight just to carry his own body. If he had, he certainly wouldn't have desired it.

Illiaz wondered what it was like to be so strong, and what it was about that which distressed Lux as the incredible heaviness of Illiaz's bones distressed him.

"Whether something is light or heavy doesn't say anything about any inherent quality of that thing, Lux, but about one's ability to carry it."

Lux blinked at him, eyes matching his jewelry: gold, carnelian, and obsidian. "I suppose that's true."

He glanced up at the ceiling for a moment, then back at Illiaz. "Then I am clearly capable of carrying more than you're giving me."

"You are." Illiaz laughed, because he figured that nothing would ever be able to weigh Lux down. "If I gave you the entire world, I'm sure you'd be able to carry it." His body was trembling, and no matter how he tried, he couldn't quite still it. He stared down at his clenched, shaking hand. "But I'm selfish, and I want to keep some things all for my own. For as long as I can."

He didn't want to share his suffering; it was his and his alone. It shouldn't belong to anyone else. Nobody else should be made to carry it, not even Lux.

But even if he'd wanted to, Illiaz could not give Lux his muscle-fatiguing, existence-wearying exhaustion; he could not give him his bone-deep, mind-flaying pain.

It didn't matter anymore, but still he covered his mouth reflexively with his hand to hide the blood in his laughter. He was so close to his death: it was all inside of him, filling him, closer than even a lover. It was all aching to *become* him, to *complete* him, to make it so there would be no more emptiness anymore inside him.

Was this any better, in the end, than if Lux had been left in the dungeons and had rotted away there, out of his mind with agony and starvation and unaware of any sense of self? Was it any better that Lux had been with him all this time, relatively free and unrestrained, if he wasn't going to remember it?

Who were they, if not for who they'd become because of their experiences, their memories? If they weren't going to remember— what did any of it matter, then? Their ephemeral feelings, their ephemeral pain. Their ephemeral lives.

Illiaz's mother's words were fluttering through his head.

"Your father and I love you, Zaz. You know that, right? We love you so much."

Illiaz did know. Had always known.

One loved others not for them, but for oneself. Illiaz distanced himself from Lux not because he believed that was what Lux wanted, but because it was what he himself wanted.

After all, if Lux wouldn't take what he wanted, then he must have not cared about himself enough. If he said nothing, it was not Illiaz's fault. And it wasn't like Lux would be any the wiser, since he'd just lose his memories again.

Whether any of Lux's time with him had any meaning, Illiaz wasn't sure. He wondered, at times, if the fact that he was so willing to take what others were willing to offer him meant that he cared about himself a great deal. Perhaps, because everything was so difficult and painful for him, he had to care just to exist as more than a sufferer. But for Lux, since everything was so easy for him that he didn't even have to try, there was no reason for him to care about any of it, no reason for him to care how he came across to others. He would always be impressive; he didn't have to fight just to be more than an object of pity.

Not that Illiaz had ever been that to Lux, but somehow that made him want to leave even less of a pathetic impression on the gladiator. How would he ever be able to stand it, if Lux changed the way he looked at him?

Lux was gazing at him, candlelight catching on the sharp teeth in his grin, the evidence of Lux's own eventual death poking through the skin of his gums, and Illiaz couldn't help but wonder, when Lux died, if it would be as a man or a monster. What would he see when he looked at himself in a mirror, at those sharp teeth and bloodshot eyes? What would he perceive of himself when he saw all the myriad invertebrate appendages that crawled beneath and broke out from his skin? When he realized that he could stomach nothing but human flesh?

Illiaz wondered if Lux would have the capacity to understand why he had still appreciated his company. Why he had wanted Lux not to hurt because of him, enough that he hadn't even asked if Lux would have preferred the pain.

Lux was looking at him, and his smile was utterly careless, his eyes dark abysses, eternally accepting of everything that fell into his fathomless gaze. He took Illiaz's breath away and made him forget, for that brief moment, all the pain of existence.

When the agony crashed back down, it did so like a cloudburst, and Illiaz drowned in it. There were no words for his feelings, which were overwhelming; no words for his thoughts, which were dizzying. The laughter rose up in him like daffodils through cold, winter-frozen earth, blossomed from his mouth and burst out like daring, taunting things.

Ah, he was dying. So much agony, and yet it was funny. Who knew dying could feel as phenomenal as this?

Lux was hovering above him, a dark silhouette edged with flame-gold.

Illiaz covered himself with his makeup and Lux covered himself with gold, both trying to make themselves into things that they weren't: dazzling enough to appear as more than a fast-approaching death; weighed-down enough to be treading the earth like a living being.

Illiaz's lungs were trying to scrabble up out of his chest, dragging up blood like chains. Illiaz coughed it out, tried to stem it with his fingers.

Lux looked so lost, his gaze fallen to the floor where the flickering candlelight made the shadows leap and dance. In contrast to that frolicking light, the accursed gladiator's expression was utterly dead and still. His voice, when he spoke, was shadow-soft.

"So what am I to you, Illiaz?"

"...What are you to me?"

It was the mirror of the question that Lux usually asked, and Illiaz wondered why that was: why Lux usually inquired not into his own role to Illiaz, but into Illiaz's role to him; why he now asked the opposite.

It was hard for Illiaz to think clearly through the pain devouring him from within. Luckily this question wasn't hard—he knew the answer already, was already painfully aware of it.

"You're all that's kept me from killing myself for years, Lux. The only reason I'm still alive. The only reason I still *want* to be alive."

Hot liquid dripped down his cheeks. He thought it was tears until he wiped at it with the back of a hand and saw that it came away streaked dark with blood.

He didn't have long left, did he? Crying blood like his mother had.

"If that's the case..."

Lux was suddenly above him, all dark shadows and glittering edges of firelit gold. He was pressing against Illiaz's chest with a hand, making even more blood cough up from Illiaz's lungs. His eyes were red and hungry, his pupils dilated. His voice was breathy: a vibrating, cicada-like purr in his chest. "What would you let me do to you, Illiaz?"

Illiaz couldn't remember the last time Lux had been fed. Illiaz's vision was becoming a mass of darkness. Only the brightest gold-lit edges of Lux and his jewelry were visible through it.

Illiaz smiled. It was all that was his choice, in this moment, and he relished it. "Anything you want to."

He was going insane with his pain—and if Lux was going insane with his hunger, then who would be losing out if Lux ate him? Not either one of them.

Lux's hand tightened hard enough around Illiaz's throat where it had moved, and the pain of it flared above the rest of Illiaz's agony. Lux's voice, when he leaned down, was arid and hissing in his ear, a spider-scuttling murmur, the weight of his necklaces crushingly on Illiaz's chest, the heat of his skin burning Illiaz through the thin fabric of his clothes.

"Even if it ruins this carpet?"

Oh, that was genuinely funny. Funnier still because now that Lux mentioned it, the blood that would get all over the carpet was indeed the only thing that disturbed Illiaz about being eaten.

"...I can't believe you, Lux." Illiaz was delighted, in that moment, to still be alive. Even gasping on every breath as he was, blinking desperately from sight.

Blood in his mouth, his nose, his eyes. The deities' laughter in his ears. His pain was beyond comprehension and Lux was a gold-edged, bright-eyed silhouette in his darkening vision. In his ears, just barely audible over his laughter, was the shivery clinking of Lux's jewelry. Then the weight of it left Illiaz's chest, along with the burning of Lux's skin as the Accursed pulled away from him.

"I know you'd willingly let me destroy you, Illiaz. But what if instead I leave you?"

Frigid, deathly coldness. Illiaz struggled to push himself up. Was Lux threatening to leave? He wouldn't be. He'd never chosen to, despite the countless opportunities. Even if he did try, he wouldn't make it; there was sunlight edging the curtains, filtering in from outside.

Lux wouldn't leave him, and through shudders of pain and the thick saltiness of blood, Illiaz smiled at him.

He was almost dead, and there wasn't any point in wanting anything anymore. And yet he still *wanted;* he still wanted *desperately.*

Illiaz laughed. Or maybe he sobbed. Or maybe it was both. The deities had gone quiet in his ears, and he wondered, idly, if they were even capable of feeling such things as affection. As care. As desire.

Was that how his parents had felt, bringing him into the world and raising him despite his illness that caused him unending agony? They'd loved him, and yet the existence they'd given him was nothing but suffering. And had that made them happy? To see him struggle so hard to pretend that he was something other than absolutely miserable?

Lux had looked at him like he was more than superficial beauty, more than inner suffering, and Illiaz couldn't help but wonder what it was that he'd seen. What it was that had made Lux relax his guard and regard him fondly, with neither reverence nor pity.

What was it, exactly, that had drawn them together? That had kept them from splitting apart, despite everything?

Illiaz didn't understand it, and he didn't think that Lux understood it, either.

It was sudden, the way Lux cut through the liquid darkness to embrace him; it made Illiaz gasp. Lux's arms wrapped around him and pulled him close, skin burning him up like Illiaz had jumped into flame. It was by reflex the way Illiaz tried to curl in on himself, and he found himself clutching Lux back as a result, burying his face against the accursed gladiator's chest even as he felt like his flesh was being seared from his bones, coughing blood against Lux's skin.

"I'm sorry." Illiaz was choking, crying tears and blood. *"I'm so sorry."*

"For what?" Lux's voice was smooth, even, unruffled.

Illiaz didn't know what he was apologizing for. Perhaps it was for all that he'd put Lux through that Lux wouldn't remember. Or perhaps it was for the fact that Lux wouldn't remember. Or perhaps it was for the fact that he was dying and he felt insane. Or perhaps it was because his deathly body must be burning Lux with cold. Or perhaps it was merely because he was coughing blood onto Lux's skin. Or because he wouldn't be there should Lux ever need him.

Lux had his nose buried in Illiaz's hair and laughed breath like lava against Illiaz's neck.

"You've admitted yourself that there's nothing that can hurt me and there's nothing I'm incapable of carrying. So it's not hurting me any if you make me carry this."

It made Illiaz laugh, dark blood and pale chunks of flesh like maggots crawling over Lux's skin, and the accursed gladiator didn't even flinch. He pulled back just enough to look into Illiaz's eyes. His enlarged black pupils outlined with thin lines of gold iris in the blood-red of his sclera were intense and hungry, but his lips arced ever so slightly.

"You're sick, Illiaz."

Blood and lung-flesh in his mouth, so thick he could hardly speak. "Yes."

Lux's dark gaze following the blood dripping down Illiaz's chin, then crawling back up the blood trails to burrow into his bleeding eyes. "You're dying."

"Yes."

Illiaz was laughing and wondering how there was any blood left in his body. The garish, viscous red was ugly against Lux's gold jewelry and bronze skin. Illiaz wanted desperately to wipe it away, but his sleeve did nothing but smear it and spread its taint wider. Like an infection. The effects of poison or a disease.

"You've been dying for a long time."

"Yes."

Lux had never minded all the gore he ended up covered with at the end of every gladiator battle, had flicked it from his fingers but otherwise exited the ring with it drying over his flesh. As if it didn't even itch. As if he wouldn't later have to soak all his jewelry and then scrub clean all the crevices with a soft, fine brush.

"So that's why you were never scared of me."

Of course that was the only thing Lux was concerned with. Lux, no matter his incarnation, had always been under the impression that he was an entity to be feared, hated, or both.

"I suppose so."

Lux looking down at him, exhaling hot, humid breath like a lethargic summer wind over Illiaz's sepulcher skin. "Is this why you wanted me here? So that I could kill you."

"It wasn't the only reason..."

"But it was one of them." Lux's tone was heavy like a headstone, and Illiaz's laugh was scattering like the falling petals of left-behind funeral flowers. White lilies splattered with red.

"So what if it was?"

"You could've told me."

Lux's voice flowed darkly over him, his fingers through Illiaz's hair tickling like the undulating of millipede legs. "I would've known my purpose, then."

Illiaz was so tired. Everything hurt so terribly. He didn't really believe in anything, anymore. "If I'd told you, would you have remembered?"

"Probably not."

"See?"

Weak and with insides that didn't want to remain within his body, pain everywhere as they tried to get out. The agony of it all was enveloping him like dark waves from a drowning sun.

"I just wanted..."

Illiaz sighed, smiled against the accursed gladiator's chest with the confidence of a secret taken to the afterlife. "My life has never been my own, Lux. So I at least want my death to be." His hand was heavy as lead as he raised it to rest blood-slick fingers against Lux's cheek, his head even heavier when he lifted it from Lux's chest to meet those butterfly eyes with a blood-flowering smile. "Would it be okay if I asked you to kill me?"

His death was pressed up close beneath his skin, yammering to break through, splitting the tissue-paper flesh of his face, of his body.

Lux's fingers on his neck were burning yet gentle. "Is here fine?"

Lux's fingers traced over his throat and Illiaz smiled, feeling simultaneously the most beautiful and the most ugly he'd ever felt in his life. "Thank you."

Love was an unfathomable thing.

Lux leaned in close, his hot breath on Illiaz's neck.

"Smile, my dear Zaz."

As Lux tore out Illiaz's throat with his teeth, Illiaz's mother wrapped her corpse-cold arms around him from behind, falling with him into the abyss.

Part III: Arianth and Philamon

ARIANTH HAD ONLY wanted to help her brother and her kingdom.

She was five years younger than her brother, and she didn't remember the Great Calamity. She'd been too young at the time, only a child of three years. Their parents had died during the tragedy. Her brother, Morphioce, had been eight years old when he'd become king.

Arianth had grown up watching her brother carry the weight of the entire world on his shoulders.

She'd just wanted to help.

Her brother hated the deities more than anything. He blamed them for the Great Calamity and sought to defy them. Rather than relying on the deities for divine Blessings, he had a team of scientists trying to figure out how to awaken magical powers in humans through other means.

Arianth had been only eleven when she'd snuck into the lab and drunk one of the potions. She'd heard the scientists talking to her brother about needing human test subjects, and she'd just wanted to help. She believed in her brother and what he was trying to do.

The magical substance turned her hair from white-blonde to deep purple, and it granted her a power that allowed her to control others with her voice when she spoke the names they held most closely to their souls.

The power also made her sick and weak in body, the ability eating away her life force.

"You *idiot*," Morphioce snapped at her, his hands gripping her shoulders painfully. "What did you do that for?!"

She was crying. "I just wanted to help you."

HIS NAME WAS Philamon Fonhellansicht, and he hated his life.

The Fonhellansichts were rich and had managed the King's treasury for dynasties, but Philamon found the elite to be full of fakes and sycophants. So he ran away.

He ended up in the village of Niran and studied the martial art of stratva under the tutelage of Aodhealbhach Sinngan. Then he spent years traveling between kingdoms, adapting to different cultures and customs, making friends and acquaintances. He saw the need for a trade network and established one.

He had reached the age of 31 when he finally returned to Mythus with his fortune. He had matured and realized the ignorance of his youth, was getting older and realized the desire for a home to come back to between trade ventures.

It was upon his return to Mythus and its elite society that he met Princess Arianth at one of the king's banquets.

In all his travels, he'd never before seen anyone with lilac hair.

It was that, first, which intrigued him.

"My name is Philamon Fonhellansicht," he introduced himself to her, bowing low.

She smiled at him, more radiant than anything he'd ever seen. "My name is Arianth, but you may call me Ari. Do you mind if I call you Amon?"

It was only later that he learned about her power—her Blessing and curse and the reason she called everyone by nicknames. At that time, he was simply telling her stories about his adventures, watching the way her blue eyes lit up with delight, her hands flying to her mouth as he told her about the dangers he'd braved, the wondrous sights he'd seen. She had the most beautiful laugh he'd ever heard, the most dazzling smile.

She enchanted him.

IT MADE ARIANTH happy when Morphioce let her use her power on advisers and ambassadors to help him. Even though it ate up her lifespan and caused her pain, she was happy. She wanted to help him carry the weight of the kingdom so he was not alone.

She hadn't expected to fall in love.

Philamon was different from the other men Arianth had met. He was more mature, more worldly, more genuine. His stories and his gifts delighted her, and he made her feel safe.

When she realized she was in love, she started sobbing.

"What's wrong?" Morphioce asked her, holding her and wiping away her tears. She felt terrible for troubling him—he had so much responsibility—but she told him about her love for Philamon. The happiness and the pain it caused her.

It was Morphioce who set up their marriage.

"You've done so much for me, Ari. You deserve happiness."

And, marrying Philamon, she was indeed happy. Even though her entire existence hurt, she was so incredibly happy. Not only was she able to help her brother by manipulating the elite of the kingdom and other lands using her Blessing, but she also had a husband who was the wisest and kindest man she'd ever met, who brought her gifts from all over the world.

The only thing that would make her happier was a child.

Philamon, making love to her, treated her more gently than anything. When Ari told him that she wanted a child, Philamon was afraid. He didn't know if she'd survive it. He didn't want to risk her death. He didn't want her to undergo even more pain.

But he couldn't stand to see her cry or look forlorn. And due to his trade company, he was often gone, and he didn't want her to be sad and lonely. So he acquiesced.

He was so afraid to hurt her. But she wrapped her arms around him, kissed his jaw and told him, "Everything hurts me, now—so go ahead, hurt me a little bit more. I want you to."

Pulling back, she placed a hand against his cheek, smiling up at him. "And don't you dare apologize. Not ever."

Philamon turned his head to kiss the palm of her hand and clenched shut his eyes against their dry sting.

He just wanted her to be happy. He'd go to the very ends of the world to do so—so how could he deny her this?

"Amon," she whispered. "Please don't make me use your full name."

Ari always got what she wanted.

ARIANTH AND AMON HAD A SON. The boy had Arianth's Blessing and cried more often than not. But he was beautiful, and he made Arianth happy.

"I love you, Zaz. I love you so much."

She didn't believe his existence to be any different from anyone else's. Every existence came with its blessings and its curses—every life came with its pain and its wonders.

She hushed her son as he cried and brushed the violet hair out of his eyes. "Hush, Zaz, there's no need to cry—Papa's gonna bring you presents from a distant land. Won't that be nice?"

"But it hurts, Mama. Everything hurts."

"I know, Zaz. I know. But it's okay. You have a marvelous power—you'll be able to have everything you want in the entire world. It will all be yours. Everything under the sun and the moon and the stars."

Her Zaz cried and buried his head against her, and she held his burning body to her cold one and sang to him, brushing her fingers through dark hair that would one day become as light as her own.

What did it matter that he wouldn't live long, when for as long as he lived, he'd have the entire world? He was so much more fortunate than all those other children out there who lived in poverty or with the barest necessities.

Her Zaz would live a Blessed life where he had absolutely everything.

PHILAMON HADN'T REALIZED that having a child could make him so happy. But it did.

Watching that child grow, teaching him, regaling him with stories of his travels that made Illiaz's blue eyes widen with wonder, that made the child laugh with delight.

The boy was beautiful, like his mother.

Still, as the boy grew, Philamon couldn't help but notice a difference between Illiaz and Ari—on their views of pain.

Ari had told him how she'd received her Blessing, and Philamon, regarding the two of them as Illiaz cried and Ari hushed him, couldn't help but think there was a profound difference between choosing pain and having been born with it.

"This pain is a Blessing," Ari had told him, content.

But Philamon, watching Illiaz bravely struggle not to cry, couldn't help but think that to Illiaz it was a Curse.

The only time Illiaz used Philamon's first name was when he was being racked by pain and Philamon tried to help. At those times, Illiaz would say: "Philamon—*leave.*" And Philamon could do nothing as his body turned and left the room.

"Don't you dare apologize to him," Ari said. So Philamon bit back his condolences and instead brought Illiaz all the wonderful presents he could find.

"Thank you, Father." The boy was dazzling when he smiled.

Philamon hadn't known that having a child could bring him

such happiness.

Illiaz's life was filled by pain, but he was strong because of it, and that made Philamon proud.

He just wanted both Ari and Illiaz to be as happy as possible for as long as they lived.

ARIANTH'S BODY WAS FAILING HER, and everything hurt more than ever. But still she was so blessed. She had her brother, her husband, her son, all of whom she loved more than anything. She didn't regret a single choice she'd made.

Her dear Zaz was sitting next to her bed, holding her cold hand in his burning one. She was so happy for her blessed life that she was crying. Her tears were running red.

"Do you want me to end it quickly, Mother?" her dear Zaz asked quietly. His other hand, clenched in a fist, was trembling.

Arianth shook her head, smiling as she gazed at him.

She didn't want to lose a single moment with him.

Her son had been doing his own makeup, recently, since she could not, and it was slightly messy around the eyes, but he was still so lovely. Arianth was sorry to leave him, but she was content knowing that he had a father who also loved him more than anything and that he would be able to get everything in the world.

In her last moments, Arianth was proud of the legacy she would leave behind in her son.

PHILAMON WAS SORRY to have not been with Ari in her last moments, though he'd known that it was likely to happen. Her death made his heart cramp in his chest.

But he still had his son, and he never would have imagined how great a comfort that was. Having this child in whom he could see both himself and Ari.

Quietly, Philamon asked him, "How were her last moments?"

"She was crying," Illiaz said, "but she was happy."

Hearing that eased some of the ache in Philamon's chest. "Are you okay?" he asked his son.

Illiaz had smiled at him, dazzling. "I'm well, Father."

They had all known that Ari was going to die.

"I'm sorry I wasn't there," Philamon said.

Illiaz shook his head, still smiling. "Don't apologize, Philamon."

It was like a lightning strike through Philamon's body; he was never able to apologize to his son again. That was how powerful was the Blessing Illiaz had received from his mother.

Illiaz always got everything he wanted. Whether that was coming with Philamon on his trade ventures or housing one of Mythus's most famous gladiators—whatever he wanted, nobody could deny him.

"I hope you'll watch over him," Philamon said to the gladiator, Luxanthus.

"Of course," the monster-killer said.

Nobody who met Illiaz could keep from caring for him. Illiaz made every room brighter simply by walking in, made the entire world brighter with his smile and gentle laughter. He was so much like his mother: it was impossible to look away from him, impossible not to hang on his every word, impossible not to want the best for him. Even the most powerful gladiator in all of Mythus bowed to his softest tone.

He was, however, still weak in body; he couldn't have held back monsters whose names he did not know. Philamon became ineffably grateful for Luxanthus's presence when the Second Calamity occurred. Despite the flood of monsters, Luxanthus kept Illiaz alive—even at the cost of his own humanity.

That was how strong was the spell which Illiaz cast over everybody.

"Lux saved me," Illiaz told Philamon later, fingers curling weakly in the blankets of the bed in which he lay. "But he became an Accursed, and then they killed him."

Philamon hated seeing his son like that: curled up in bed, dead-eyed and refusing to eat.

"Why am I still alive? I should be dead."

Those words made Philamon's chest ache more painfully than anything.

He just wanted his son to live happily despite the pain of his ability.

Investigating what had happened to Luxanthus, Philamon discovered that the gladiator was still alive, but that he was locked away deep in the dungeons. According to the guards, he kept breaking his way out.

"Bring him to us," Philamon told them.

If anyone could control the gladiator-turned-monster, it would be Illiaz.

Philamon wanted to see his son smile again. Seeing the life return to his son's expression would be more than worth housing a monster. More than worth the delivery of corpses. More than worth the broken statues and the damaged walls and floor.

"I hope you'll watch over him," Philamon said to the gladiator-turned-monster.

Luxanthus blinked at him with his bloodshot eyes and said, "Of course." Even a monster couldn't help but fall for Illiaz's charm.

Illiaz may have been weak in body, but his power over others was incredible.

It was only after Luxanthus went wild from stepping into the sun that they found Illiaz's body, mostly devoured. It made Philamon exhale all the breath from his lungs.

"It looks like he failed," said the captain of the anti-Accursed unit, but Philamon shook his head.

"No," he said, "Illiaz asked for it." If Illiaz had been eaten, it was because he had desired to be.

Illiaz, like his mother, had always gotten what he wanted.

Philamon watched as the new King of Mythus fought the monstrous Luxanthus and subdued him. This king was not white-blond with blue eyes like Arianth's brother, but had golden-blond hair and red eyes. Like Illiaz and Arianth, he seemed somehow more than human.

"Hm," the king said, a hand over the accursed gladiator's face, "how much would you like him to remember?" The king was glowing, as if lit by sunlight from within.

"At least let him remember Illiaz," Philamon said.

Luxanthus may have become a monster, but he had become one in order to keep Illiaz alive; he at least deserved that much.

King Gamesh nodded and glowed more brightly.

Once he was done, Luxanthus stood, blinking at him. He was standing in the sunlight, but he was calm.

"What do you remember?" King Gamesh asked him.

Luxanthus, with his bloodshot eyes, looked at him and said, "That Illiaz told me to live."

King Gamesh nodded. "Very good," he said. "How would you like to become my warrior?"

As the king left with Luxanthus following him, Philamon, despite the pain of loss, couldn't help but feel glad that Illiaz had gotten what he wanted.

What a magnificent world it still was, where people like Ari and Illiaz, even despite all life's curses, could live lives that were so blessed.

PART IV: LUX

"I WAS ALWAYS TOLD TO LIVE LIKE A ROSE," Illiaz said to him, fingering the stem of one of the delicate flowers in its vase. "Roses decay. You should live like gold, Luxanthus, and never fade."

"Gold is metal," Luxanthus pointed out. "It's not alive."

"And yet," Illiaz said, smiling like an unfurling bloom, "both roses and gold are considered beautiful."

That conversation ended up being the only thing Lux would remember.

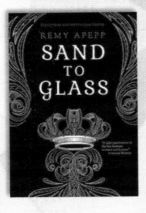

TRAPPED BY CRIME. FREED BY MAGIC.

When Skate tries to burgle a shut-in's home, she gets caught by the owner—a powerful undead wizard. He makes a deal with her. Now, she'd better find out exactly where her loyalties lie.

Skate the Thief
by Jeff Ayers

TRUE LOVE. ANCIENT CURSES.

Theodora is determined to unravel the mysterious Seth Adler's secrets. No matter how many thousands of years old.

Painter of the Dead
by Catherine Butzen

RIDICULOUSLY MAGICAL. MAGICALLY RIDICULOUS.

Crafted as a slave to serve Time, the clockwork man escapes to seek out his imagination, his purpose, and his name.

The Land of the Purple Ring
by Deborah J. Natelson

IT'S TIME TO TAKE OVER

Fodder of Humble Village is a soldier for the plot of each new story, and, frankly, he's really sick and tired of getting speared, disembowelled, and decapitated so the good guys can look glorious. In fact, he's not going to take it anymore.

The Plot Bandits
by Katherine Vick

AND YOU THOUGHT COLLEGE WAS TOUGH BEFORE

Try getting bitten by a werewolf. And being hunted by madmen. And being stalked by a very suspicious secret organization.

Hunter's Moon by Sarah M. Awa

THE CLOCK IS TICKING

Plans seldom survive contact with the enemy, a truth thrown at Mercedes when an ordinary trip turns into a battle for survival.

Bargaining Power
by Deborah J. Natelson

ABOUT THE AUTHOR

REMY IS FOND OF understatements. Some of Remy's favorite understatements include the following:

Remy likes writing.

If stories were stars, Remy would want to write an entire night sky full.

Remy writes stories for the same reason explorers adventure into and chart unknown territories—and also for the same reason people treat headaches by drinking water, eating snacks, taking pain meds, going for light walks, and getting rest.

All Remy wants from life is to write stories that touch you in the same place music does; that make you think differently than before; and that linger in your mind as if they'd been written into clay tablets rather than printed on paper or typed on screens.

But ultimately, Remy just hopes that you enjoy/ed this book.

73055657R00113